I0649318

W. S. Lach-Szyrma

Aleriel; or, a Voyage to Other Worlds

A Tale. Second Edition

W. S. Lach-Szyrma

Aleriel; or, a Voyage to Other Worlds
A Tale. Second Edition

ISBN/EAN: 9783337246730

Printed in Europe, USA, Canada, Australia, Japan

Cover: Foto ©Andreas Hilbeck / pixelio.de

More available books at **www.hansebooks.com**

ALERIEL;

OR,

A VOYAGE TO OTHER WORLDS.

𝔄 𝔗𝔞𝔩𝔢.

BY

REV. W. S. LACH-SZYRMA, M.A.

VICAR OF NEWLYN ST. PETER,

AUTHOR OF

"A VOICE FROM ANOTHER WORLD;" "A SHORT HISTORY OF PENZANCE," ETC.;
"HEROES OF THE DAY;" "PLEAS FOR THE FAITH," ETC. ETC.

WITH MAPS OF MARS AND VENUS.

_____

SECOND EDITION.

_____

LONDON:

WYMAN & SONS, 74-76, GREAT QUEEN STREET,

LINCOLN'S-INN FIELDS, W.C.

1886.

All Rights Reserved.

PRESS NOTICES.

———•◦•———

" The book is curious, and not a little mystical."—*Bookseller.*

" We hope the tale will have the success which its merit fully deserves."—*Literary Churchman.*

" This very fantastic tale has been written with a fixed purpose."—*Notes and Queries.*

" The story is very skilfully and ingeniously told, and as a speculation in science is consistent and not improbable."—*Yorkshire Post.*

" Portions of the book remind us of Swedenborg, Fontenelle, and Lord Lytton . . . . The story throughout, however, is curious, and very well told."—*Liverpool Mercury.*

" No ordinary reader will rise from its perusal without enjoyment, and without having gained in a most attractive form a better knowledge of the wandering stars."—*Western Daily Mercury.*

" The author never offends, and the moral lesson inculcated is a good one."—*Lloyd's.*

" The author has allowed his fancy to have free play, while his speculations are based on the known facts of Astronomy, and he has imparted a moral and religious tone into his amusing and somewhat fantastic tales."—*Church Times.*

PREFACE TO THE SECOND EDITION.

I AM, on the whole, pleased with the reception of this little book by the literary world. It has received less adverse criticism than I anticipated. The serious side of the book, the underlying theory of the Cosmos, has, however, not generally been noticed. Although seemingly light and imaginative, this work is the result of many years' study of Nature's laws, and my meditations upon Creation have led me to a theory which I have only ventured to lay before the public in this popular and imaginative form.

This theory is that life is well-nigh universal, and that, as we see the elements (in the spectroscope) which are found upon the earth, prevailing in distant stars in divers combinations, so the forms of life which are found on earth, prevail in other worlds, but under various kinds of development. At present, man knows of two worlds of life—the Land and the Aquatic, to which we may add the worlds of past ages in Palæontology. But, both on land and sea, we find the same general conception (so to speak) of flora and fauna. The sea has its plants (in the algæ), its moluscs, its insects (in the crustacea), its vertebrata (in the fishes and cetacea). So in past ages life, both by sea and land, seems to have been complete: plants, insects, vertebrate animals existing even in secondary formations.

Let us now by the symbols A, B, C, D represent the four great types of life.

A. Vertebrata $\Big\{$ *again in the Vertebrate Animals* $\Big\{$ AA. Mammalia.

B. Articulata   ...   .   AB. Birds.

C. Mollusca   ...   ... $\Big\{$ AC. Reptiles and Amphibia.

D. Radiata and Zoophytes   ...   A.D. Fishes.

In Plants $\Big\{$ A. Dicotyledons.   C. Ferns & Cryptogamous Plants.

B. Monocotyledons.   D. Algæ.

Now, may not these types be found on other worlds, distributed and developed according to the fitness of their habitats? I have supposed the type :—

AB. in *Mercury*, which is similar to Venus in many ways. (With this I have not dealt in this work.)

AB. in *Venus*. Mountainous ; dense atmosphere ; moderate gravitation ; varied climates, suited to birds or flying beings, able to traverse space easily ; plants, perhaps monocotyledons.

AA. in *Earth's Land.* (Perhaps with element of B for man as a biped, has some slight corporeal connection with both the quadrumana and birds.)

AD. in *Earth's Ocean.* Fish type and Algæ.

AC. in *Earth in ancient state* in secondary formations. More marshy, therefore reptilian and amphibious types prevailed.

AA. in *Mars.* Moderate atmosphere ; few mountains ; surface, mostly land. Mammals, like carnivora.

AD. in *Jupiter.* Great gravitation; surface, mostly fluid. Plants, algæ. Animals of fish type.

AC. in *Saturn.* Antique world, like Earth in secondary epochs. *Uranus* and *Neptune* as yet little known in their physical formation.

This is the conception of Nature I have thought of: Unity in Diversity, but all showing the same Divine Law-giver; life developed under the same laws, and united in its higher forms to rational intelligences, like Man.

PREFACE.

WHEN children are shown the wonders of the heavens, for the first time, in the telescope, their natural exclamation usually is, "Are there any people up there in those planets?"

It is an old question, and the affirmative answer is rather supported than overturned by the discoveries of modern science. When we are told that everything almost that we can see on Earth—yea, every particle of dust—has once lived, we are inclined to think that the same law which seems to be the dominant law of Earth, *i.e.*, that nearly all things on Earth's surface either have lived or are now living, may perchance be the general law of the universe.

Our Earth is singular in nothing. In size, the giant planets Jupiter, Saturn, Uranus, and

Neptune are much larger; Mercury, Mars, the
planetoids, and the satellites much smaller;
Venus, our twin-sister world, almost the same.
In form, the Earth is nearly a sphere, and so
are all, or nearly all, its fellow-worlds; some are
more flattened at the poles, and some less.
The Earth is enveloped in an atmosphere,—so it
seems are Venus, Mercury, Mars, and probably
the giant planets Jupiter and Saturn.   The
earth has continents and oceans,—so have Mars
and (probably) Venus. The Earth has snow in
winter,—so it seems has Mars.   The Earth
possesses a satellite,—so do Mars, Jupiter,
Saturn, Uranus, Neptune possess their satellites.   In fact, the Earth is peculiar in nothing
which we might expect to trace in other worlds.
Why should we suppose it to be the sole abode
of life? This subject has been much discussed.
Not to speak of the older astronomers, in our
own time Proctor, Flammarion, Brewster, and
Powell have discussed it.   I must own that the
objections have ever seemed to me to be most
frivolous.   Can this grain on the sands of
infinity—this little planet of an unimportant
system—be the sole abode of vitality?

But, if there be life, what life? This is a
question which has occupied many of the
noblest of human minds. Man cannot know

absolutely, in this his Earth-life, what the life of other worlds may be.

> On Nature's Alps I stand
> And see a thousand firmaments beneath,—
> A thousand systems as a thousand grains;
> So much a stranger and so late arrived,
> How shall man's curious spirit not inquire
> What are the natives of this world sublime,
> Of this so distant interrestrial sphere,
> Where mortal untranslated never stray'd?*

Probably the best conception of this matter is that suggested by Messrs. Nasmyth and Carpenter, in their valuable work on the Moon, where they say, "Is it not conceivable that the protogerms of life pervade the whole universe, and have been located on every planetary body therein?" In the Moon, circumstances seem to be unfavourable to life; but it is a mere begging the question to assume that this is the law of every orb in heaven save this earth of ours.

In the following tale or speculation (as you choose to take it), although apparently I have given no rein to the imagination, yet I have endeavoured to avoid as much as possible any conflict with established scientific discoveries; and, indeed, have based my speculations on the

* Young.

known facts of astronomy, only allowing the fancy to have free play where science is, and must be, unable, in its present state, to answer the questions here considered. If there are any statements which are found to be irreconcilable with any of the recent discoveries of inductive science, I shall be much obliged to any scientific reader to draw my attention to them, and they shall be corrected in a future edition.

It will be noticed by the reader that, to give it more human interest, and also to ventilate some practical subjects, there are two Utopias in this book—the one in which there is a speculation as to a perfect society of perfect happiness, such as may be regarded as a meditation on the possible joys of a future state; the other a more practical Utopia, implying the tendencies of human progress, and suggesting improvements for human society as it now exists. The other worlds beside these two (Venus and Mars) have no special earth-lesson to teach; they are little more than bold deductions from observations or probabilities suggested by them.

I have by no means assumed, as some extreme partisans of the habitability of other worlds are wont to do, that all the planets are inhabited. I rather suppose that Earth at present is merely an example of one phase of planetary development, *i.e.*, one in which life can exist; that some worlds are like it (though none in precisely the same condition); that others are as yet in a primitive state, just as the Earth was in the period of, say, the secondary formations; that others, however, are more highly developed than this world; and, finally, that in others life is extinct. This ideal is much the same as that of Oersted, who says: "On some planets the creatures may be possibly on a far larger scale, on others far smaller, than on our own; on some, perhaps, they are formed of less solid matter, or may, indeed, approach the transparency of ether; or, on others again, be formed of much denser matter. The rational creatures on some of the planets may be capable of receiving far quicker, more acute, and more distinct impressions than on the Earth. We may imagine that there are reasonable beings with weaker faculties than our own" (as I have in these pages supposed to be the case); "but, if we properly appreciate our present distance from the aspirations of our reason, we feel compelled to acknowledge that an endless number of degrees of development may exist above the point we have reached."

I have further supposed that no two worlds
are alike in their developments of vitality, just
as no two are alike as seen in the telescope,
nor in their apparent physical characteristics.
Yet, as in all the solar system there is an
underlying unity of design, so I have supposed
that "unity in diversity" is the law of vitality
as well as of matter, and thus that the life in
each of our sister-worlds is like some form or
other of life to be found on Earth, just as the
fact has been revealed to us by the spectroscope
that the same metallic and gaseous elements
as we find about us on Earth exist even in
distant stars.   Thus I have supposed that the
life in other worlds is like what we find on
earth, but that in each world there is a distinct
development.   In the apportionment of each
such development to divers worlds, I have supposed that the physical constitution of each
world, as far as we know it, affects the form of
life upon it.

As to the theological question of God's deal-
ings with the inhabitants of other worlds, I
have hardly presumed to touch the subject.
These things we can only know when we see
no more as "in a glass darkly, but face to
face"; and it seems to me that those who have
ventured to speculate on it, as Kircher or
Swedenborg, have exceeded propriety.

The pessimism of my hero also requires some apology. I appeal, however, to my reader's intelligence, whether any one coming from a happier world, and seeing the anomalies and misery of Earth, would not be shocked and pained? As it is, the pessimism of Aleriel is not stronger than that of the Wise King in Ecclesiastes, nor of many ancient and modern philosophers. It is not nearly so bitter as that of Byron.

With regard to the resemblances to other works of this character, *e.g.,* Swedenborg, Fontenelle, Lord Lytton, &c., I may say frankly that I have not copied, consciously at least, from any one. If resemblances occur, they may be attributed to the fact that two minds have come by diverse paths to the same conclusion, and that conclusion has therefore something to be said for it—which is all one can say for an obscure speculation of this nature.

The fabric of the work is a continuation of my "Voice from Another World," a short *résumé* of part of which I have given in the Trehyndra letter, to make the argument plain. I must add that the *dramatis personæ* are, of course, purely imaginary.

In conclusion, I must ask my readers to consider the work as a whole, and not condemn

it entirely if they find some one passage opposed
to their preconceived notions. I can hardly
expect any one to agree with me in all points.
I trust, however, that this seemingly fantastic
tale may encourage the young to study in more
serious works the facts of astronomical science,
and perhaps cheer their elders with the thought
that, though much is sad on Earth, yet there
may be brighter worlds than this, and a happier
existence than we can have here. Earth is not
the Universe, and our life here is not eternity.

CONTENTS.

—◆◆—

PART III.—MARS.

PART IV.—THE GIANT WORLD.

PART V.—SATURN.

Part VI.—CONCLUSION.

NOTES.

A VOYAGE TO OTHER WORLDS.

PART I.—CHAPTER I.

THE HUNCHBACK OF MONT ST. GABRIEL.

IT was a lovely morning in the June of 1870, when I left the little town of B——, in Brittany, for a walk to the neighbouring hill of Mont St. Gabriel, where there was a celebrated old chapel, commonly counted as one of the sights of the neighbourhood. I had just left Oxford for the vacation, and was refreshing myself, after a term's hard work, by a walking tour in France. My companion, Galton, had sprained his foot, and was staying at the hotel resting himself for the day, but I was unwilling to miss this opportunity of seeing Mont St. Gabriel; so I started on the morning's walk of some four kilomètres alone.

It was a quiet and somewhat desolate route, and many thoughts about the past and future

B

and eternity came unbidden before my mind.
But I need not trouble my readers with them,
for they have little directly to do with my
story ; they were, however, afterwards indelibly
fixed on my memory.

I at length reached the little promontory
running into the sea, on which Mont St.
Gabriel stands. I climbed over some rocks
which bounded the path and made my way up
to the picturesque and antique chapel, now
ruined. The view was splendid. The blue
sea adorned here and there by little ridges of
silver foam, the wild rocky coast, the crying of
the sea-gulls, and the low roar of the ocean,
all tended to awe me, and then to quiet my
mind into a calm reverie.

"How beautiful is this world!" I thought.
"I wonder if there is anything that can exceed
in loveliness such scenes as these, or the
glorious Alps, or the splendid rough Cornish
coast in a storm, or the lake districts of the
north. This world is very beautiful."

I am afraid I must have been giving way to
the bad habit I sometimes have when quite
alone of talking to myself, for suddenly I was
aroused by a slight rustling behind me. I
turned, and a very singular-looking person met
my gaze. He was a very short fair young

man, greatly deformed about the shoulders. He was dressed in a common *ouvrier's* costume, with a large Breton hat and a cloak thrown over his blouse. His face, however, in spite of his coarse costume and manifest deformity, was of exquisite refinement and even beauty. His complexion was fair as a girl's, but pale even to bloodlessness. His eyes, though somewhat obscured by the hat, were most strange and brilliant. His features small and delicate. He had neither moustache nor beard, and scarcely looked above twenty. He was gazing at the sea, and though near me appeared not to notice my presence.

For several minutes I remained silently looking at the waters, with, I must own, an occasional glance at my companion. "Poor fellow," I said to myself; "what a singular malformation about the shoulders. I never saw anything like it before. And, then, how deadly pale he is, and so refined, in spite of that peasant's dress. Perhaps he is some gentleman in distress; some unfortunate student who has failed in life's battle." And then a dreadful thought seized me. "I hope he is not meditating suicide, or he is not mad. In either case I am in an awkward position in this lonely spot, in a strange country, with a madman or one in utter despair."

But when I looked again at that strange meditating face the thought was dispelled. He was thoughtful, but not at all sad; nor was there either the excited or the sullen look of mania about those intellectual eyes. But still he looked on, silently watching the sea.

I was immensely puzzled, and was getting quite uncomfortable, for Galton had been entertaining me the evening before with a whole series of horrid Breton legends about the " White Lady," and the ghosts and the signs of death ; and really here was a personage who, if he had been met at night, might have been easily taken for a *revenant.* But it was not night, and the sun was shining brightly, and the shadow of this stranger's curious figure was clearly defined on the chapel wall.

At last I thought it was useless and un- courteous to thus pretend not to heed him, and that it would be better to speak. So I broke the silence with a polite bow and a " Bonjour, monsieur."

" Good morning, sir; you are English, are you not ?" he said, in a very sweet and clear contralto voice, and a singular but pleasing foreign accent.

" Yes," I said, " and am very glad you can talk with me in my native language. May I ask also if you are French, or a stranger to this country ? "

" Un étranger, monsieur," he said in French, and then relapsed into silence.

So it was evident that he knew both French and English, and was neither French nor English. What countryman was he ? The voice, the accent, and the manner were as strange as the appearance of my new acquaintance, and gave me no clue.

My question seemed to have silenced him, and, for several minutes again, he appeared to have no wish to renew our conversation. At length I broke the silence.

" You speak English well for a foreigner. Have you ever been in our country ?"

" Never, sir, but I much wish to visit it. I have been told it is a land of liberty and progress, that there is much that is noble and good in your country. There is a great deal that is sad to see in other parts of Europe— misery, oppression, and sorrow. I should like to see a happier land in this world. Perhaps England is such—perhaps it is," he added, after a pause. " They say your country is rich. I hope that the many have the benefit of that wealth, and not the few."

"I am afraid we cannot say that. There are great disparities in England as in other lands. How do you like France? I may ask you; for you say you are not a Frenchman."

"A gay, pleasure-loving nation, wanting in gravity, in stability, in religious sentiment. France lives too much for the present and not enough for the future—not enough in the past. It is selfish and proud, and pride oftentimes precedes a fall. The Latin races seem growing effete. They have had their day. The Teutonic races may have the present and the immediate future. However, I cannot tell. The state of Germany is sad, though not as sad as France."

The intelligence of his remarks touched me. I looked down at his worn and almost ragged trousers. It seemed to me sad that one so intelligent and educated should be a mere peasant and in want. After some momentary misgivings, as I rose to return to B——, I resolved to do something to aid him. I put my hand in my pocket, and, blushing, offered him a five-franc piece. "My dear sir, perhaps you want this more than I—pardon me in offering it." He took it, smiled, and simply said : " Thank you, sir ; if I can return your kindness I will. We may meet again."

"Adieu," I said, " I hope we may meet again."

I bowed, and left him still standing gazing on the sea.

CHAPTER II.

BESIEGED IN PARIS.

I WENT up to Paris by the next morning's train, Galton, whose foot was much better, accompanying me.   His walking tour was necessarily terminated by his accident, and so, as I did not wish to lionise Brittany alone, we resolved to stay a little while in Paris together. The gay city looked gay as ever—bright, cheerful, and frivolous.   How few in those two millions dreamt of the catastrophe hanging over them, an unseen Damocles' sword suspended by a hair in the midst of all that gaiety and splendour.   I am sure I as little foresaw the peril to Paris as any one, nor, still worse, the catastrophe hanging over myself.

    *   *   *   *

One morning, just as the papers were getting excited about the Spanish succession question, I thought it would be a pleasant change to have a trip to Versailles.   Galton had gone off to Brussels that morning, so I was left alone.

I little dreamt of what that little trip would cost me. We had just got to near Sèvres station, when, in a moment, I heard a tremendous crash, the panels and roof of my carriage fell in masses about me, and amidst the screams of the passengers, the wounded and the frightened, I felt a sudden blow and then an intense agony in my leg, and then ——

*   *   *   *

I will not dwell on that painful time at the Hôpital de S. Clotilde. I was put in the accident ward, and must say that I shall ever feel grateful to the careful and kind nurses and doctors who attended me. My injuries were tedious and painful rather than dangerous; my leg was fractured, and the shock of the accident had shaken my nervous system.

While in the hospital I heard the patients one day talking of a remarkably able young doctor, whose wonderful cures were attracting great attention in medical circles. I listened with avidity to these stories, and resolved directly I was able to consult him.

In a few days I was well enough to be removed to my hotel in the Rue Pelletière. Here, directly I was ensconced in my own chamber, I wrote a note to Dr. Posela (the young doctor of whom I had heard so much in the hospital) asking him to come and see me.

In about a couple of hours after my note was sent, the *garçon* announced Dr. Posela.   He entered, and, to my astonishment, I beheld again my deformed little friend of Mont St. Gabriel. He was now somewhat better dressed, but, though the day was warm, was wrapped up in a cloak.   There was the same soft, strange expression on his face—a peaceful repose—and yet a *je ne sais quoi* of mystery and solemnity about him.   He was surprised as well as I was.

"I am glad to meet you," he said, "and yet sorry to see you thus.   You suffer, I fear. Oh! frail humanity.   What man has to go through in his earth-life!   I wish I could make you well at once, but what you say in the report of your case you have enclosed in your letter shows me it is just a case where I can do least.   A broken limb!   Only nature can cure that.   But I can relieve your pain."

He then questioned me on my symptoms, and, on leaving me, gave me a potion which marvellously relieved my nervous depression.

*   *   *   *

Day by day news became more anxious in the political world.   The war had broken out. The march *à Berlin* had commenced, and the shouting had even reached us when I was in the hospital. Now the papers formed an occupation for my thoughts even in my sick-bed. Posela's treatment gave me wonderful relief; but the broken bone needed rest for cure, and I had to stay in my room a prisoner while the busy and memorable scenes of the war— Gravelotte, Mezières, Sedan—were exciting the minds of every one around me.

I saw nothing of Posela after that visit. I learnt that next day he had started with an ambulance in connexion with the army of Marshal MacMahon.

I was really beginning to get very anxious. I at length quite recovered from my illness and was able to get about; but the line of "blood and iron" bound me, like every one else, within the besieged city. There was no lack of excitement indeed. The news of every day was thrilling, and one often saw terrible scenes of war. It was like being a spectator of a vast tragedy, and the Parisians viewed it as such. Their strong dramatic sentiment was excited and almost amused, at first, by the spectacle of war at their very gates. I could not resist the contagion; but still I had a good deal to be anxious about, as they had. My autumn term was hopelessly lost at Oxford, of course, and possibly my Lent term would be also, for it looked as if this siege would go on for a long time; indeed, the Parisians declared they would hold out to the last. If so, my prospects of getting away were bad indeed, and I was in danger of this wretched Franco-Prussian War doing a permanent injury to my career.

*   *   *   *

I remember one evening walking along the Tuileries gardens watching the flashes of the Prussian artillery, and seeing the French troops marching up to the ramparts, with their drums beating before them. The cannon were roaring as a thunderstorm, and yet the Parisian crowd was looking on calmly, as if merely witnessing a tragedy, instead of themselves being in a beleaguered city. Suddenly I noticed Dr. Posela passing close by me.

" Where are you going ? " I said.

" To the ramparts. I must do my best for the wounded. Oh, it is a terrible war! How can men ever carry on and systematise this horrid mode of settling national differences? Hark! how the cannon are roaring! Many a soul is being launched into eternity. How terrible! How unfit are some to go! "

" You take it more to heart than most

around you. But you are in danger in the front."

"Do not trouble yourself about me; think of yourself and of the poor soldiers; I am in no danger," and he smiled.

"Yes; but you are in the front. The cannon kill doctors as well as combatants. It is really a dreadful system of war—this long range. It is almost worse than the hand-to-hand strife of the days of chivalry. Every one suffers. I heard only yesterday of a shell bursting in a bedroom of a school where nine little boys were sleeping, and killing three. I only wish I could get out of the city, for I have nothing to do with this quarrel."

"Perhaps not. However, let us have a talk again to-morrow. *Au revoir!*"

I went home to my hotel, and as I woke in the night and heard the distant roar of the cannon, and saw the flashes through my window-blind, I thought once or twice of brave, kind Posela, and his errand of mercy in the ramparts.

CHAPTER III.

THE ESCAPE.

NEXT morning, just after my late *déjeuner* (of a rather limited and not luxurious character, for food was getting terribly dear in Paris, and the horses were beginning to be doomed to the slaughter-house), I was starting for a lounge in the Rue Rivoli to hear the news, for which every one was almost as eager as for dinner, when I met my eccentric friend.

" How have you fared last night ? Will you come in and take some refreshment ? "

" I cannot take anything ; but I should like to speak with you."

We went upstairs to my bedroom. Posela sat down and looked at me fixedly, in a way that somehow made me very nervous, for he had a wonderful fascination about the eye. I never felt any one's eye like his.

" Do you really wish very much to get out of this terrible place; to go home to your peaceful country from these horrid scenes of war ? ''

" Indeed, I do ; I would pay almost any price, short of doing a wrong action, to get out of it. What is it to me? I am not a Frenchman ; this is not my country. I have no interest in this quarrel, and, if I had, I hate war ; I always have hated it, and now more than ever. It may develope manly qualities, but still it is an evil thing at the best."

" You really wish to get out of Paris ? " he asked.

" Why ask ? Is it not clear that I must wish to get home ? My whole future may depend on it. If I lose another term my chances of honours are gone. Do, in God's name " (for I was getting excited), " tell me how I can get out."

" I cannot do that ; but I can get you out."

" How ? "

" I must not say how. But by to-morrow morning, if you wish it, you may be on your way to England. Only, you must promise me never to ask how I have freed you."

" I promise you. I give you my word—I will give you my word of honour as a Christian, and as an English gentleman—I will never ask

you, if only you engage that it is by no wrong
or dishonourable act that I am passed out."

"I can assure you of that. There is no
harm in my mode of liberating you and myself.
For I must go with you to England; that is,
if you like my company."

"My friend, my liberator, how shall I ever
be able to show you how grateful I am?
Perhaps, if you come with me to England, I
may strive to show you a tithe of my gratitude.
But how can we get out?"

"Hush! you have promised."

"Pardon me; it was so natural an exclamation. When will you come to take me
away?"

"At eight. Be ready; but I can only take
you, not your property; that must be left.
Adieu!"

I can scarcely say how delighted I was at
the prospect of deliverance. The condition
seemed curious; but I was too glad at the
hope of escape to trouble myself about it.

*   *   *   *

I packed up my things and locked my
portmanteau, and asked my host to take great
care of it when I paid my bill, and to let me
have it when the siege was over.

"But, monsieur, you cannot possibly pass

the Prussian lines. They will not let any one through, I assure you, not even an English-man. You will be shot, monsieur."

" I cannot tell you how I can get out ; but a friend says he will manage it, and, as he is a very clever fellow, I am too glad to believe him."

" Perhaps it may be by a balloon ; but there will not be any balloon going for three days."

" Well, I must be off. So please take care of my portmanteau, and I trust you will be spared in this terrible siege."

" Ah, monsieur, c'est vraiment terrible," said mine host.

I went off, bidding good-bye, with a light purse,—hardly enough left for my journey to England.

I hurried on to 17, Rue Soubise, in Mont-martre, where I knew Posela lived. In answer to the *concierge*, I was directed to the fourth *étage*, where I knocked at a humble-looking door just as the clocks were striking eight.

" *Entrez*," said Posela's soft, sweet voice.

I opened the door and entered. It was a quiet, unpretending little room, but with a fine view over the city, most of the lights of which were clearly visible from the window. There was hardly any furniture, and what there was

seemed poor.   It looked a mere *ouvrier's* room.
In front of the open window was a sofa.

"Are you sure you wish to leave Paris?"

"I am quite sure, believe me.   My money is
nearly gone, and my patience also.   My life
may soon be in danger.   I assure you I shall
be deeply indebted to you if you set me
free."

"Then, sleep!"   As he said that, he made
a sort of mesmeric pass over me with his hand.
I felt my senses dulled, an oppressive drowsiness overcame me, I sank upon the sofa, and
was soon buried in a heavy sleep.

*   *   *   *

How long I slept I know not; I think it
must have been three or four hours.   When I
awoke I at once saw that I was in a totally
strange place.   It was a large field near a
chaussée, with a wood close by.   Not a human
being was to be seen.   Everything was still
and calm, and the air was fresh and chilly.   It
was the repose of the country.   I got up and
stared about me, but the light was insufficient
to make anything visible, except the indistinct
outline of the trees and the greyish-white stones
of the *chaussée*.   I turned.   In the distance
behind me was the haze as of the lights of a
distant city.   I paused and listened.   Yes!

far, far away was the dull roar of distant artillery. I was out of Paris.

The thought of my sudden release quite overcame me. I fell on my knees and thanked God for my deliverance, which was so sudden and inexplicable as to seem almost supernatural. How could I ever have passed that line of "blood and iron"? What means could have been used. At any rate, Posela had kept his word. I was out of Paris and beyond the Prussian lines at last, and nothing remained between me and England but a train and steamer journey of a few hours.

As I was walking along the *chaussée*, still uncertain where I was, or where I ought to turn my footsteps, I suddenly noticed a man seated on one of the white stones that marked the border of the road. He was crouched down; but, even in the darkness, I thought I recognised Posela.

" Is it you, Posela ? " I said.

" Yes."

" Well, I am greatly obliged to you for your successful fulfilment of your promise. But where are we? We are out of Paris, that is clear ; but where are we ? "

" At Pontoise. Do you not see the lights of

the city? Hark! there is the boom of the cannon!"

"At Pontoise? Let me see; that is a station on the line to Amiens. Let us get to the railway, and proceed to England by the first train."

Posela assented, and we walked down the hill. In a quarter of an hour we were entering the town and passing down its silent streets, quite deserted, save by the Prussian sentries, whose helmets glistened in the gaslight. I now beheld them for the first time. It was evident we were out of the lines of Paris.

We found the railway-station lighted up, and half full of people waiting for the early train. A Prussian sentry was walking up and down, and a corporal's guard were lounging in the *salle d'attente.* At length the train came up, and I can hardly describe my feelings when at last I was on my way to England.

My strange travelling companion was rather sad. He spoke again and again of the miseries he had seen, caused by this terrible war; of the folly of nations in not abolishing such a mode of settling disputes; of its waste and sinfulness. I listened to him, and accepted his arguments, which were eloquently put. Then he changed the subject, and asked me a host of questions, many of which I could not answer, about England ; about its history, government, population, natural products, climate, &c. As we talked, he took out a note-book, and seemed to be taking down what I said. I was rude enough, I fear, once to look over his shoulder ; but, though a fair proficient at shorthand, and a student not only of the phonographic but other systems, I could not detect what it was he was writing.

At length we came to Dieppe, which I found in possession of the Prussians. In a few hours I once more trod on British soil.

"How delighted I am," I said, "and how grateful to you for bringing me home to dear old England ! "

"One loves one's country. I suppose I should love mine, even if it were less lovable."

"But what is your country ? "

He was silent, and seemed not to hear my query.

CHAPTER IV.

LONDON.

IN a couple of hours we were at London Bridge. It was already morning—a cold wintry morn, but not so foggy as usual. We had no luggage to carry, and my purse was nearly empty; and, really, Posela seemed to have nothing, for I had paid his fare and my own, and he seemed utterly to ignore the fact, a point of eccentricity which at another time I should not have quite liked; but which, under the circumstances of my deep debt of gratitude, I could not complain about, so I suggested we should walk to my home in Kensington. As we crossed the bridge he seemed much struck at what he saw; at the crowds and the shipping. He leant over the parapet looking at the Thames.

"This, then, is the greatest city upon earth?"

"Not merely the largest that is, but that ever has been. Not even Imperial Rome was ever as great as London is. It has nearly four millions of population."

" That is truly great. Four millions ! That is more than Sweden, or than Denmark, or than Greece ! "

" Much more," I replied.

" Do you think it is for the happiness of such a number of people to be living altogether in one city ? Have they enough light and air ? Is it always smoky here like this ? "

We talked on thus as we walked through the City. He showed keen interest in everything, and often varied his questions by sage and thoughtful remarks. His character throughout was very strange; he seemed full of sympathy for human sorrow, and yet he was not dazzled by anything. He seemed curious, and yet when he saw a thing was disappointed, and spoke in a tone of sadness and pity of everything, showing how it might have been better, and ought to have been better than it was. It was, in a sense, disappointing to show our great metropolis to so severe, though, at the same time, so kindly, a critic. He evidently sincerely pitied us, pitied London, pitied England, pitied everything and everybody, and yet, strange to say, he was not conceited, not self-opinionated, not misanthropic. He appeared, however, to look on everything from an exalted standpoint, saw every imperfection, and yet did not rejoice at seeing it. I tried with patriotic zeal to set everything in the best light before my kindly, though mysterious, benefactor, but it was useless. He evidently thought us in England a very unfortunate race of beings, and London a very large, but by no means a grand, city. I remembered his remarks at our first interview, and was sorry to find his expectations of England were disappointed.

We thus came to my home. My father was, I need not say, delighted to see me. I had written from Pontoise, and posted my letter just before leaving; but I had come faster than the post. The family had only heard of me by balloon post some weeks before, and now I was come, most unexpectedly.

"How did you ever get out, my boy? I understood the Prussians would not let any one pass their lines. I suppose you were favoured as an Englishman?"

"By no means. How I got out must remain a secret; in fact, I do not understand it myself. However, all I can say is, that I owe my safety entirely to Dr. Posela, whom I must now present you as my best friend and deliverer."

" Well, sir, I am happy to make your acquaintance, and am too glad to see my son in safety to be too curious to know how you evaded Prussian vigilance. Are you a stranger to England ? "

" I was never here," said Posela, " till this morning; and yet I have often looked on England from afar, and wished to be there."

" From Calais, I suppose. One can see the white cliffs of Albion in fine weather there."

Posela made no reply.

The conversation changed. A flood of queries gathered round me. The breakfast-bell sounded, for it was still early, and we went into the breakfast-room. When he had finished his questions to me, my father naturally turned his conversation to our guest, and I noticed at once how much he was impressed with him. On the war he had very little to say, all questions on it appeared disagreeable; but on every other topic he talked well. Still, he was by no means one who wished to lay down the law, or to show his talent. He rather excelled in question than in reply ; but his questions showed a *naïveté*, a thoughtfulness, that was striking. He asked upon almost every topic connected with England—its history, government, politics, statistics, religion, commerce—

everything. My father was a man fond of giving his opinion on things, and so he was delighted with his intelligent and thoughtful guest. Some things Posela seemed to have a difficulty in comprehending, especially how there could possibly exist so much misery in such a wealthy land, and how people could differ so on religious topics. The government by parties confused him, as well as the existence of unchecked immorality in our great metropolis. After breakfast we went out to see London, my father accompanying us. We saw as much as we could in that day. Posela took an interest in everything, but was a rapid sight-seer. In most things he took in what he saw very quickly, and I thought was rather inclined to hurry. The sight which struck him most was the British Museum, where we stopped some hours, and he here especially took interest in the ornithological department.

In the evening, after our long sight-seeing was done, and I was thoroughly tired (although I had accompanied them to scarcely half the sights), Posela inquired how he could get to America, as he wanted to visit Niagara, and then to proceed to San Francisco. We found that one of the Cunard steamers was to sail in a couple of days, so it was resolved that he should proceed with me to Oxford after another day in London, and thence go to Liverpool to embark.

This programme was carried out. He spent another day's sight-seeing in town, a portion of which he insisted on giving again to the British Museum, where he studied some of the curiosities with keen interest. In the evening we went to a festival service at one of the London churches. It was, he said, the first time he had an opportunity of attending a Church of England service. He had talked to me on religious topics two or three times, and always expressed himself with the utmost reverence. Indeed, he seemed of a highly devotional type of mind, though of what form of Christianity he was I could not tell; he was certainly not an Ultramontane,. nor did he seem a foreign Protestant. Once or twice I thought he belonged to the Greek Church, but really of this there was not much evidence.

At the service he behaved with the utmost reverence, and joined in the singing with a rich and wonderfully melodious contralto voice (it was far above a high tenor). He seemed to throw himself utterly into the service, and appeared wrapt in devotion. When it was

over, having said my private prayers, I prepared to go, but Posela remained kneeling.
I waited and waited. Every one, except the
attendants, had left the church, but Posela
remained in an attitude of prayer. At last I
had to touch him and whisper, "The service is
over, and they will want to put the gas out
soon."

"Over; and so soon! I thought this was
merely the preliminary. How soon men are
tired of prayer and praise!"

CHAPTER V.

OXFORD.

NEXT morning we started together by an early train for Oxford. On the whole, my singular friend appeared more pleased with the university city than I expected ;—the number of public buildings, the grouping of the architecture, the gardens, the museum, the libraries.

" I rather like Oxford," he said, after a few hours' hurried walk about the colleges and "the lions "; " If I had time I should wish to stay a day or two here. It reminds me ——"

He paused and did not finish the sentence.

" At any rate stay the night," I said. " You are really not doing justice to the city, and I should like to introduce you to some friends."

I had, indeed, asked some of the reading set to which I belonged—all quiet, studious men, going in for honours—to my rooms to coffee after dinner. Posela consented to stay another day with me, and dine with me.

My friends were warm in their reception of

me, and full of questions about my adventures
in the siege. I soon noticed, however, that my
strange companion attracted their attention.
Quiet, unassuming, and retiring though he was,
there certainly was something so singular in
his manner, appearance, and mode of speech,
that one could not help observing him. Hilbert,
a Merton man, with whom I was very intimate,
and who had joined our party, was especially
fascinated by him. Hilbert was an eccentric
man, who was chaffed a good deal for his
credulity in mesmerism and spiritualism. He
and Posela were greatly drawn to each other,
and were soon on Hilbert's favourite topic—the
occult sciences.

" I am convinced," said Hilbert, " that there
are two ruling forces in this world at the
present day. Money and Psychic force. Of
these I am by no means sure that the latter
and least accepted is not really the most
potent; for the man possessed of psychic force
can compel those under his influence to give
their money as he wishes by will - power.
Many of the great men of history have been
so, not so much by reason of their mental en-
dowments, as by reason of this psychic force.
See Napoleon I.—how marvellous, almost
supernatural, was his career; and a great deal

of it was due to his will-power over men. In destroying authority, and in weakening the power of kings and priests, we have given these two forces—money and psychic power—unbounded range. As long as authority existed, the rich man might be restrained in the use of his wealth, and psychic force had also its limits. Now, more and more, man deals with man in the battle of life; thus the richest and strongest gain supremacy."

"True," I said. "I see this most markedly in the religious movements of this world. How marvellous is the devotion of some of the sects, who profess so strongly to believe in private judgment, and the rights of liberty of conscience for their leaders and preachers. I can only account for this by psychic force. All revivalism partakes of it. A revival is a kind of *séance*, where spirits are invoked who possess the converts. Only the worst is, that the theory is that these mesmerised patients are hereby sanctified. It is only a sort of deification of psychic force."

"What do you think of this matter?" asked Hilbert of Posela.

"Psychic force," he replied, "is indeed a motive agency in the history of mankind. It is useless talking of liberty as long as weak

men submit unquestioningly to the commands
of other men of stronger wills than their own,
even to their own injury. It is one of the
marvels of this world, and one of the secrets of
the possibility of the wretched government and
misrule we see, that men so blindly submit to
one another's will, and then talk of liberty."

As we had been just talking of spiritualism,
I suggested a *séance*. I was not much of a
believer in it, but I knew Hilbert professed to be
a medium; and I thought at least, if there was
anything in it, that this might be a way of solv-
ing the secret about my mysterious friend,
without asking him questions. I rather
thought he objected to the *séance* at first, but
at length consented to join the circle. We
half turned down the lights, and laid our hands
on the table in the approved mode. In a few
minutes Hilbert gave symptoms of drowsiness,
and then appeared to be slightly convulsed, the
usual symptom of what spiritualists call " being
under control." A sheet of paper and a pencil
had been laid on the table under a cover.
" Take off that cover," said Hilbert. I did so,
and on the paper was traced these word :—

" We cannot reveal anything to-night. There
is one in the room whom we cannot understand,
but who looks very different to us from what he

does to you. Perhaps he knows more than we do."

Posela did not like this message. He rose from the table and remained nearly silent for most of the evening. Next morning he started for his American tour.

CHAPTER VI.

A LOVE CHAPTER.

SIX months had passed. To me it was one of the most eventful periods of my life. I had gone in for my degree. My honours were not so high as I had once hoped for, as my Paris adventure had thrown my reading back terribly. I took a second, however, and found some of the brilliant and fresh thoughts of my mysterious friend of value to me in the examination. " We have had to examine you for a first class, for some of your answers were so remarkable," said one of the examiners to me afterwards. " Where did you read these extraordinary ideas ? "

" I never read them," I said, " I only heard them from a very singular and eccentric genius whom I met in Paris. I think they seemed true, though where he got them I cannot say."

*   *   *   *

After leaving Oxford, I went as private tutor

to a young man called William Richardson, the
son of a rich shoddy plutocrat, of Manchester,
who wished his son to go, under an Oxford
tutor, on a tour through Europe. As I knew
France fairly already I was especially fit for
this kind of work. Our tour, however, extended beyond France into Switzerland and
Germany. We went to Strasburg, thence into
the Schwarz Wald, where we took a charming
walking tour for a few days. We took train
at Freiburg for Bâle, whence we walked
through the region of the Juras to Berne.

At Berne we met a charming family, a
father, mother, and daughter,—the Christo-
phersons—to whom I had introductions from
some college friends. I found Mr. Christopherson a most agreeable acquaintance, and
one who especially suited my tone of mind.
We often took excursions in the mountains
together with young Richardson, sometimes in
the company of the two ladies, who drew out
very pleasantly the intelligence of my young
charge. I must say I was, at first, somewhat
jealous of the notice Miss Christopherson took
in Richardson, but I soon saw that she merely
patronised the raw lad, whom I think she
rather despised than admired, though, in kind
good-temper, she sometimes brought him out.

Those walks and rides round Berne—in the sight of the glorious snowy Alps, or by the brawling Aar—I never shall forget. They are among the brightest parts of my life. Several times I referred to my mysterious friend and deliverer, Posela, from whom I had not received any letter or communication since he had left for America.

"I so wish you could meet him," I said one day, as we were walking on the hills near Berne, to Maud Christopherson. "Perhaps you could find out his mystery. They say ladies are sharper in detecting secrets than men are."

"I should, indeed," said Maud, "like to make the acquaintance of your mysterious friend. A man who can pass a friend out of Paris in the midst of the siege through the Prussian lines, —who has such wonderful powers of putting people to sleep when he wants,—who is so learned on every subject and yet so young,— such an admirable Crichton, who never will tell anything about his nation, or origin, is indeed a curious person worth meeting. I rather like eccentric people. Your friend seems like Joseph Balsamo of Dumas' novel; but I hope he is not such a rascal."

"No; I am almost sure, mysterious though

he is, that he is no rascal. He seems religious in his way; though what his religion is I cannot detect. He speaks most reverently of every phase of Christianity, and appears in conduct to be quite consistent. His manner at St. Anselm's church was most devout, and as for the fashionable scepticism of the age he always spoke of it with ineffable contempt, as even more silly than wicked; for, again and again, he urged to me that piety was true wisdom."

"Perhaps he is a hypocrite," said Mr. Christopherson, breaking in on our talk. "I do not like these mysterious folk. He may be a Nihilist, or head-centre of the Fenians, or some such dreadful thing."

So we often talked over Posela, and the more I spoke the more the ladies seemed— excited by curiosity—to wish to meet this strange being, so different from everybody else.

*　　*　　*　　*

One morning, when I came down to breakfast, I found a letter in a strange, but fine, hand on my table, addressed on from my college at Oxford. It bore the Bombay postmark. I broke the seal, and was both surprised and pleased to read the following :—

"Bombay, —— , 1871.

" DEAR HAMILTON,—I expect to be at Berlin
at the entry of the Prussian troops in triumph,
If you should be there, I should be glad to
meet you.   I shall be in the Unter den Linden,
on the left side of the Brandenburg Gate.   May
God be with you.

"POSELA."

I showed this strange epistle to the Christo-
phersons.   The ladies were charmed.
" Do let us go to Berlin," said Maud.   " I
should so like to see the entry of the Prussian
troops.   It will be a sight we can never see
again.   It will be seeing a great historical event,
to be talked of ever after."
Although I suspect that the charm of the
Prussian entry was only a part of their reason
(for they had never talked of this long journey
to Berlin before), yet their entreaties were so
earnest that Mr. Christopherson yielded, and
together we proceeded through Germany to
Berlin, just reaching there the day before the
triumphant entry.

*   *   *   *

I need not attempt to describe this splendid
military spectacle, so often told by abler pens.

Suffice it to say that it exceeded our expectations. We took our stand close to the Brandenburg Gate. The crowd was so dense that it seemed like looking for a needle in a bundle of hay to look for Posela there; but, as the Guards swept past in serried array, on lifting my eyes to a tree, I noticed there my singular, eccentric friend. He saw me also, and made a sign of recognition. Keeping my eyes fixed on him, I noticed, before the procession ended, that he let himself down, and was lost in the crowd. We remained where we were, and in a few minutes Posela elbowed his way to my side.

"I thought I should meet you here, although the crowd was so great. I am glad we have found each other."

"So am I," I said. "Allow me to introduce you to Mr. Christopherson. Come and dine with us at our hotel—the Hôtel de l'Europe."

Posela accepted, and we hurried through the crowd to the hotel. At dinner I put many questions to him about his journey. He had been round the world, and seemed to have seen everything. He had been in California, Peru, Australia, New Zealand, Japan, China, India, and Egypt. He had climbed Chimborazo and several Mexican mountains. He had sailed up

the Hoang-ho and Yang-tze Kiang. He had
visited Siberia, and had scaled the giant mountains Everest and Dwalighiri. At first, evidently,
Mr. Christopherson was not agreeably struck
by him. I saw that, as a man of the world, he
suspected Posela of boastfulness and untruth-
fulness. In fact, he evidently did not believe
he could have been in all these places, especially
in so short a time. As for Mrs. Christopherson, she was certainly amused, and somewhat
pleased to have a chat with so great a traveller.
Our conversation naturally turned to the
pageant of the day. I asked Posela what he
thought of it.

"I never saw anything like it of the kind
before. I do not admire it, for, as you know,
I do not like war. And yet courage and
endurance are virtues, and, perhaps, such
pageants are needed to encourage men to be
brave and enduring."

We stayed till late in the evening talking
over many matters. As before,—indeed, more
than ever,—I was struck with Posela's varied
information, the freshness of his thoughts, his
brilliancy, depth, and acumen. Many of the
ideas he expressed I had never heard before.

"Will you give me a recommendation to
some friend of yours in England," said Posela,

"who is living in a country place? I want to have a little rest in quiet."

"Oh, yes. I am sure S——, one of the fellows of my college, who is now Vicar of Trehyndra, in Cornwall, would be glad to know you. We often talked of you at Oxford, and he wishes much to make your acquaintance."

I wrote him a letter of introduction, which he took.

*　　　*　　　*　　　*

"What do you think of Posela?" I asked of Maud next morning.

"I do not altogether like him sometimes, and yet I think he ought to be liked. There is a something uncanny about him. Sometimes, really—do not laugh—he hardly seems like a human being at all. His eyes are so wonderful and uncanny, his voice so singular,—his marvellous learning,—his apparent youth. Really, he seems like the 'Wandering Jew' or the 'Flying Dutchman,' or something else supernatural. I feel quite afraid of him."

CHAPTER VII.

A STRANGE LETTER.

MONTHS had passed—eventful months for me. One of the events my readers may guess. Our sympathy about Posela and his secret had developed into sympathy in other matters. There was a mutual approachment between Miss Christopherson and myself, which ultimately led to my suggesting to her a change of her name for mine, on which subject I was referred to her parents. The saying is, that the course of true love never runs smooth, and perhaps ours did not; but the obstacles did not prove very serious, and in less than a year from our first meeting we were joined one fine sunny morn together at the altar of St. Aldemund Church, "for better, for worse; for richer, for poorer," in the bonds of matrimony.

My readers may expect that with this *dénoû- ment* my simple story ought to end. But, in fact, we have only got through the introduction; the really important part is yet to come.

We set off for a quiet honeymoon to Oban, and there, a day after my arrival, the following extraordinary letter reached me from my friend the Vicar of Trehyndra, containing the key to the wonderful secret of the mysterious Posela :—

" Trehyndra.

" MY DEAR HAMILTON,—I have at last solved the secret of your mysterious friend ; but what a secret it is ! All your guesses were quite wrong ; but it is excusable that you never thought of the real solution of the mystery. I never should have supposed it possible, had he not told me it, and shown by ocular demonstration that his statement was true.

" As you know, I was very much interested in what you told me of Posela ; and after your letter saying he probably would visit us in Trehyndra, I looked out for a visit from him with longing expectation. No letter, however, arrived announcing the day he had selected for coming to us.

" He came to our village in a storm—a night fit for the witch scene in Macbeth. The wind was blowing ' great guns,' as the sailors say, and the sea was heaving with a succession of waves which struck in foam and spray against the shore. The storm had raged all day; but he did not come till night.

" A ship was being wrecked on our dreadful coast—an event, alas, not very rare. Posela distinguished himself most wonderfully—it almost seemed to me at the time supernaturally—in saving the crew. I did not have any interview with him that night, but next morning he introduced himself to me, and gave me your letter.

" I was charmed with him from the first. He was evidently a person gifted with remarkable intelligence and mental power, and considerable brilliancy; but of that I *now* feel no wonder.

" The only thing that seems to me marvellous is his wonderful adaptability to circumstances so different from those to which he was born, and his wondrous power of disguising his real nature. We had many and pleasant talks about numbers of subjects, and some of his remarks I remember then struck me as very strange, although I see now everything is capable of explanation. The only thing, beside the wonderful mystery hanging about him, that I did not like was his contemptuous criticism of many of the things of this world. Still he was not conceited in manner, but occasionally humble and unpretending, and seemed by no means void of sympathy.

"On the whole, I think he is the most agreeable companion I ever met, and his variety of information upon every subject is very remarkable. However, it appeared rather in generalities than in details. Upon natural science he was especially well informed, being thoroughly conversant with the most recent discoveries, and advancing many theories to explain natural laws such as I never heard before, and which I now suspect no one on earth but himself was acquainted with. His grasp of the laws of nature was truly extraordinary.

"One of his most remarkable, and, as I thought, most incongruous, characteristics was his love of children. I took him into the schools to show him our mode of teaching, in which, as in everthing else, he took an interest. He taught a class several times, and seemed wonderfully gifted in power of illustration, quite fascinating the children by his bright manner, his vivid imagination, his lucidity, and brilliant descriptive power. Especially in the geography class did he shine, telling the children about the different places on the map that he had seen, and he appeared

to have been almost everywhere. You expressed doubts, as you recollect, on the
possibility of his having been at all the places
that he said he had visited. I have no such
doubts; certainly not now, nor even had I
when I heard him give our little ones a
geography lesson.

" I even, though I had some scruples at first,
gave him a class for religious instruction, and
shall never forget it. His reverence in speaking of sacred things, his eloquence, his tender
illustrations of the love of God, were simply
wonderful.

" But he soon made friends of the little ones,
not only at work, but at play. His acrobatic
skill is marvellous, and he very soon fascinated
them by showing feats of skill and entering
into their games.

" Here was a mystery to me that I could
not at the time fathom. How could this
strange being,—about whom some marvellous
secret hung,—who appeared so profound, so
learned, and so wise,—be so popular with the
children ? I could not solve the problem. I
once ventured to ask him about it. He replied
by a question : ' Is it not wisdom to mingle
with the beautiful and the good, where we
can find them—to make friends of innocence ? '

"I feared the children would grow too familiar with him, and take liberties. It was not so, however. They soon loved him; but I thought they also feared him a little, and a naughty child was in a moment cowed and awed by a look from Posela.

"So things went on in the parish. Posela regularly attended our daily services, and appeared to be most devout. The services are humble enough, as you know, and few avail themselves of them. Posela expressed wonder at this. 'How is it,' he asked me once, 'that so few come to church on week-days?'

"'Some are employed about their work, some are indifferent to religion, and some regard it as a matter only for Sundays.'

"'But do not all your people wish to go to heaven when they die?'

"'Yes; I suppose so.'

"'Then, if they find the half-hour or so of the service of the Church on earth too much for them, how can they hope to enjoy properly the ceaseless adoration of the Church in heaven? I always am glad to go to church while on earth; it is the brightest part of my life here. I love to be in contact with my Creator and with the souls of good men. An earthly

parish church, with all its defects, is most like
of all things in this world to heaven. If one
is in sorrow, surely it is the best place to pour
our griefs to a loving Father; if in joy, it is
the best place to think of heaven.'

" I was much struck by this remark. 'Can
any one, I thought, who expresses such senti-
ments be really wicked ? He is evidently no
hypocrite. He enjoys the service greatly, and
is of a devout mind. His secret, whatever it
is, cannot be a very harmful one.'

" And still it was manifest, with all his child-
like love of childhood, with all his unobtrusive
piety, that he had some wonderful secret which
he sought to conceal from every one. His
manners and habits were strange. He loved
to walk alone on the moors; he shrank from
every question about his antecedents, save and
except about his recent voyages, on which he
was particularly communicative; he expressed
himself strangely at times, and certainly had
odd ideas.

" No letter came for him while he was
staying with me, but a large box arrived by
the parcels delivery. After it arrived he
grew more reserved, and went out on the
moors by night a good deal. I ventured once
or twice to enter his room. His box was

locked. It was very wrong of me, but I own to have felt curious about that box, for in it I knew was much that might solve his mystery.

"If he was popular with the children, he was not entirely so with the grown-up people. Our folk, though very civil to strangers, are, like most country people, somewhat suspicious of them. They noticed a mystery about my friend, and, though he was very 'free and homely' (as they called it) with them, they saw there was some secret about him. Mysteriousness engenders suspicion. Curiosity was excited. In a country place, where there is not much intercourse with the outer world, any stranger would attract attention. We need not wonder, then, at the intense curiosity, and the many surmises, aroused by Posela. Strange rumours arose about him in the parish. Our superstitious people evidently thought him supernatural, a sort of 'white witch,' for they use the term alike for men and women; but, as they believed also in ill-wishing and ghosts, I did not heed this much. However, there was one thing which appeared not to be altogether fanciful, *i.e.*, sundry lights of different colours were noted to arise on the wild moors of Penmor and upon the marshes, which were rarely traversed by human foot.

Though few people passed at night by this desolate moor, yet so large a proportion of these saw these lights that it would be difficult to believe that they all suffered from delusion. The lights seemed to come and go, to appear and disappear, but never to be seen again of the same form.   It could not all be a delusion, for the number of witnesses was so great, and yet, curious to say, no two persons agreed in their accounts of what they saw ; all saw something, but each one gave a different account.

" The subject occupied my mind, and at last I resolved, unknown to Posela, to go myself one night to investigate the matter, which I doubted not was connected with this mystery or my strange guest.

" I went out one evening on the moors with a companion, who, however, deserted me as soon as the lights appeared.   They were very extra-ordinary, and suited the descriptions of the peasantry, in being exceedingly varied in form and colour.   Several acres of moorland and swamp suddenly changed colour.   The cause must have been very powerful, as the twilight was scarcely out of the heavens, and the planet Venus was shining brightly amid the stars, giving a pale light over the country.   Still neither the vestiges of twilight, nor Venus, nor the stars were anything to these brilliant and vivid lights. One of them suddenly illumined the place where I stood, for a moment. Then I was left in comparative darkness, with the unpleasant feeling that whoever caused them must have detected me.

"I heard behind me the sound of the flapping of wings, and then suddenly I perceived, close by, a figure sitting on a granite block just in front of me. It was Posela. I asked him plainly what could induce him to come there at that time. His answer was a singular one. 'To write a letter to my friends.' This strange reply encouraged me to put the great question which had so often been almost on my lips, and ask him what was his secret. At first he was silent. I pressed him. But he did not speak. I looked at him. It was evident he was answering me in act, not in words —to my sight and not to my hearing. His eyes were phosphorescent and shone in the darkness. It appeared as if he were not a human being. Greatly agitated, I solemnly adjured him in the name of the Most High. The phosphorescence died away and he spoke. 'Let it be so!' In a moment after, casting off his cloak, I beheld a sight that I never shall forget.

It was no human being that was before me; nay, more, it was no earthly creature. His aspect still was partly human; but from his shoulders expanded huge wings, while from under his dress a most extraordinary robe was outspread. Around his head and form a sort of phosphorescence flickered, which gave him a strange and unearthly look. All I can do to describe him is that he seemed to combine the human and the bird type—not unlike the pictures we see of angels. I felt natural alarm, but he comforted me. I asked him whether he was an angel, or a spirit of one departed from this life. But he said he was neither, but only an inhabitant of another world, who had been able—first of his race—to visit this earth : that once he had been a being inferior to man, but in process of ages, not being liable to death, had developed in his far-off planet into his present condition. Having thus far satisfied my curiosity, he departed and left me alone on the moor.

" It was difficult for me at first to believe that my strange visitor was not a human being. His disguise was so complete, and he had so wonderfully adapted himself to the ways, words, and doings of humanity, that really I thought it was a mere dream, and I can well pardon you if you are incredulous on reading this.

*   *   *   *

" ' I am incredulous, indeed,' I said to Maude. ' Can it be really true that I have been travelling with, talking to, entertaining a being who is not only not human, but not even earthly.'

' Well,' said Maude, ' I do believe it. There was always something about him of the supernatural I could not help shrinking from, and yet I liked him. He seemed so good and kind, and yet so mysterious. I am sure that what you have just been reading is quite true.'

" ' But let us go on with this strange epistle,' I said, and continued reading.

*   *   *   *

" When I recovered myself I found myself alone on the moor. I thought at once it might be all a dream; that I had fallen asleep on the rocks, tired out by my walk, and dreamt this wonderful vision. I went home full of doubts, thinking over this extraordinary and unearthly scene. Was it, or was it not, a mere dream ?

" Next morning Posela did not reappear until near midday. I found him alone in my study. At once I entered on the great question upon my mind, and asked him if I had been dreaming last night. He answered, without any delay or explanation : ' You saw me as I really am, Aleriel, the wanderer, from another world, the explorer of the realms of space.'

" I was then encouraged (finding I had unawares entertained so unearthly a visitor) to ask him some questions about his world and the universe around us. He said that life was the highest primal force, and existed throughout the universe. As earth was only one of millions and billions of worlds, so man was only one of millions of forms of the higher developments of life. In some worlds they were in a lower condition than mankind, in others there were intelligences superior to man. Mankind might ultimately develope into something superior to what he is now. At first, he repeated, he was inferior to mankind; but in the peace of his beautiful world, in their loving obedience to God's laws, its inhabitants had developed a higher and a better life than man on earth, and thus had become superior to man, as they were better than man. This could account for his power of passing from one world to another, because in his world the intelligences had a far greater control over natural forces than on earth, and so he had been able to come to earth, though no human being could ever hope in earth-life to quit the earth's surface for any distance. Having told me something about his beautiful world—which I understood must be the planet Venus—he consented to show it to me in a vision. I lay down and dreamt a strange dream.

"It seemed to me that, for a time, I was in awful loneliness in space. The stars were shining in black ether over me, and the glorious sun still blazed. I felt I was in the heavens, but alone. The feeling was awful!

"It passed away soon. The bright evening star—the glorious planet Venus—rapidly grew larger and larger. At length I beheld a huge glittering globe before me and then beneath me: I felt sinking into it. Vaster and vaster it grew. Continents, oceans, mountain-chains were opening to my vision, although more than half veiled in silvery clouds. I seemed rushing to it with incredible velocity.

*   *   *   *

"Then it appeared that a huge ring of stupendous mountains, shining in the bright sunlight, were beneath my feet: I was sinking into their circle. They were of vast height; the Alps would be mere hills in comparison. Their peaks were twenty miles high at the least, and the ring was greater than a couple of good-sized counties. The lowlands were still half hidden by floating clouds. I can hardly describe that huge mountain-chain. We have nothing on earth so gigantic. Precipices of miles high, jagged peaks of shining rocks, hanging terraces clad with what looked like vegetation of many hues; soft yellows, delicate pinks, and especially pale blues.

"At last it seemed I was approaching one of the peaks. I rested there. There was no snow, though so high, and the rock was bare. It was like an earth rock, but of no stone that I had ever seen. I looked around me on that wonderful spectacle. Lines of colossal mountains, chain beyond chain, were on one side of me; on the other, an immense expanse of low country stretched in a huge amphitheatre, partly shining in the blazing sunlight, partly shadowed by the huge ranges of distant peaks—a land divided between day and twilight.

"Then my dream changed. I felt that I was slowly sinking lower and lower into that vast valley. As I sank, it appeared that the sun set amid the gigantic mountains. A vast lake lay at my feet, and in it a large island with gardens, towers, and spires of a very quaint and extraordinary style of architecture.

*   *   *   *

"Then it became night. I was walking in the midst of a vast garden. Around me were a thousand forms of dense vegetation—or what looked like vegetation—but of a sort utterly different to anything we have on earth. Our earthly words are only formed to express earthly ideas, but for these scenes of another world they are quite inadequate. One wants another language for another world of ideas. So everything around me, in earth's words, would be nameless, and, except by a long account, indescribable. Yet it seemed as if both the animal and vegetable kingdoms were there—things very different from the productions of the earth, but still not utterly of another order of being.

"The plants were various, graceful, and beautiful. Birds in thousands were fluttering in the air, some as huge as the fabled 'Roc' of Arabian fable, some small and brilliant in colour as our humming-birds. But what caught my attention most was the crowds of winged semi-human figures, like Aleriel, who moved amidst the gardens. Like everything around in this brilliant world, they were beautifully attired, in many divers ways and in many colours. There was an air of peacefulness, of cheerfulness and happiness, all around me, which seemed most charming.

"But withal there was something intensely tropical in the scene. It looked as if it were a land where light and heat and moisture were combined to develope life; everything was of most brilliant colouring, as if it revelled in intense vitality—something beyond even the tropic luxuriance of the West Indies or Ceylon.

"I noted figures of sentient being moving about in all directions amid these tropic gardens, and seemingly conversing with one another, or else listening to soft and delicious music which was borne on the breeze.

"At length I came to a palace of enormous size and most quaint architecture (quite unlike any style I had ever seen, whether Greek, mediæval, or even Indian or Chinese), airy and fantastic to the last degree; brilliant with mosaics of every possible colour; lighted up with all sorts of coloured fires and electric lights. It was a perfect fairyland.

"I entered this palace, and saw in its corridors many strange sights, such as I should never have thought of in my wildest dreams, and such as I find it difficult to describe.

" Then I awoke from my wild vision, and found my strange guest sitting by me.

" ' You have seen my home,' he said. ' Is it not lovely ? I am going to it to-morrow.'

" It was as he said. I accompanied him, at his request, to a wild part of our coast in the evening. Here I followed him up one of our cliff castles, where he mounted on one of the granite rocks, and, throwing off again his disguise, he bade me farewell. It seems that I fainted, for when I looked for him again he was gone.

" I do not know what you will think of this solution of the mystery of your singular friend. It appears to me like a dream, and probably it will appear so still more to you. As far as I can tell, however, it is nothing more than the plain truth. It would seem that (as every one almost now believes) there are other worlds than ours—worlds peopled by intelligences, some of which are superior to man. One of these intelligences has, in human disguise, visited us. That is all the explanation I can give you. He was neither a spirit nor a phantom, but an embodied intelligence similar

to mankind in nature; but not the same, as
composed of a body, not formed of earthly
elements, and of a soul not the same as our
human soul, as never liable to separation from
that body. Such an intelligence we have
received among us.—Yours faithfully,

"S——."

PART II.—INTRODUCTORY.

THE MYSTERIOUS DOCUMENT.

WE had been married some years, and were settled in our quiet little home at Branscombe, when one morning, just as I was sitting down to breakfast, Maude brought me up with the London paper, and the usual circulars, begging petitions, &c., which came daily to us by the post, a curious little packet with a Swiss postage-stamp and post-mark on it.

"I declare," she said, "this looks like a letter from our wonderful friend, Posela."

"Impossible," I replied. "It cannot have dropped from the sky. How could it have come in a meteor? Well, if we do establish a post from another world, really things have come to a climax."

"I should always have been interested in a letter from your mysterious friend; but

now, when we know his story, it is especially
interesting.   Do open it."

I opened the roll with trembling hands.
It was so strange a feeling to be touch-
ing a manuscript, not of this earth, earthy,
and written by a denizen of another world.
The first thing that caught my attention
was that it was not of paper or of parch-
ment, but of some soft and light pinkish skin,
unlike anything that I had ever seen.   It
was extremely thin, as, indeed, in the Post-
office it was only charged as an ordinary
letter; but it appeared, as I unfolded it, sheet
by sheet, to be quite a book, closely written over
with a bright purple ink.   The document was
in English, and I had no difficulty in tran-
scribing it, for Posela's handwriting, in our
characters, was clear and very delicate.

The first thing that I took out of the packet
was a small green note with a curiously ornamented border.   It read thus :—

" DEAR FRIEND,—Before I left you I promised to write to you again, and tell you about
myself.   I doubt not that you have heard from
Trehyndra about me, and who I am.   But, as
much has happened since I was with you on
the earth, I give you this narrative of myself

and my journeys since we parted. May every
blessing rest on you and yours, and may you
in time rejoice in a happier world!

"ALERIEL."

I read and re-read this curious note, and
then proceeded to read over the MS. It was,
indeed, a strange document. I could hardly
restrain expressing my astonishment in many
places, and had a difficulty in following it; but
I give it here just as I received it, hoping my
readers may have as much pleasure and wonder
as I had in its perusal. The manuscript read
as follows : —

CHAPTER I.

ALERIEL'S JOURNEY HOME.—THE MOON.

"WHEN I ascended from Trehyndra, I soon attained to regions where man could never in his earth-life exist—far above the earth's atmosphere. Higher and higher I ascended, till the whole of Western Europe opened like a map before me, with Great Britain and Ireland on the blue sea, like a brownish-green triangle on a blue field. Higher and higher still I went, till the white Alps expanded before me, and I saw the realms of Asia opening up, lightened by the dawn. On, higher and higher, till all the earth seemed a huge globe, with part light and part darkness, only varied by the cities' lights.

"As I ascended, I soon came near to one of the great meteor streams that dash through space with the rapidity of cannon-balls. I selected one large meteor, and chaining my car to it, swept with it onwards towards your satellite, which loomed as a distant globe, part light, part dark, in the black ether.

As I drew near it, in the vast realms of space, I loosened my car from the meteor, and then, restoring the power of gravitation, dashed on into the lunar sphere of gravitation towards the southern mountain-region that surrounds the lunar South Pole. It was a wondrously grand, and yet an awful, spectacle,—those vast and desolate rings of lunar mountains. Chain beyond chain, circle beyond circle, ring beyond ring, of extinct volcanoes opened up to my vision,—all glistening in the bright sunlight. To man, the heat would have been fatal. Boiling water was nothing to it. The thermometer rose to what you call 400 degrees. But our natures can bear much greater heat than that. In our own world, so near the sun, we often get it. Higher and more potent than man in vitality, freed from his lower necessities, we can flourish and enjoy a vigorous life where he would die. So the intense heat did not inconvenience me. I only dwelt admiringly on the superb spectacle—a spectacle such as I never saw before; though it was more like, in some points, the scenes on

F

Venus than on the earth. The nearest thing I can liken it to on earth is the view of the Alps from some of the Swiss mountains. I have seen something a little like it when I rested once on the summit of Jungfrau, and looked upon the chains of Alpine peaks,—on Eiger, the Wetterhorn, and far-off Mont Blanc. Peak upon peak, chain upon chain, opened to my view. But the absence of the ring-shape of the mountains marks the difference between the mountain-lands of the earth and those of the moon. In this the lunar mountains are more like ours than those of earth, though Vesuvius and the mountains of the Sandwich Isles are a little like the huge craters of the moon.

I made designedly for Tycho,—the metropolitan crater, as your astronomers call it. The huge circle of ramparts (but little lower than the loftiest mountains of Europe), in terrific precipices of a mile or more in sheer descents, opened before me. The enclosed region of the ring was larger than many an English county, but it was a vast desert; not an even plain, but rugged, with piles of rocks, relics of ancient volcanic eruptions. The central cones stood out somewhat as the Malverns stand in the midst of the plain of Worcester-

shire. Fancy the circle complete—the Cots-
wolds and Welsh mountains some ten or twenty
times more lofty—up to the level of the taller
Alps; the Malverns raised to Ben Cruachan;
the plains of Worcester and Hereford and
Gloucester a lifeless desert covered with rocks,
and you may gain a feeble conception of what
Tycho is.

All was dead around me. Not a city, not a
house, not a tree, not even a blade of grass
was to be seen. All horror, desolation, death!
And yet, withal, Nature, even in that dead
world, has a certain strange beauty.

I made for the central group of mountains,
(which I have likened to the Malverns). Here
on their southern slope I descended. The
shock was violent, though I tried to soften
the fall. I dismounted from my car and trod
another world, the third world I had visited.
It was a solemn and sublime feeling,—that of
treading a fresh world in space.

I clambered up the chief peak of the central
mountain of Tycho. Around me stretched the
desert-plain for some twenty miles on every
side, and then, beyond and above all, the mighty
ring of mountains, without a break, only varied,
here and there, by the long shadows of their
rocks.

I paused and gazed a long time on this wonderful, but desert, scene, and then, longing to expand my view, I strove to fly. But in vain. There was no atmosphere to support me, so I had to return to my car and to set its motive forces at work so as to cast off the gravitating power of the great orb about me and to float in ether over its surface. I passed over the ridge of Tycho to some four miles' altitude above the plains and crater-valleys. Again ring beyond ring of mountain circles—some glistening white, some shaded—opened to my eyes. It was a grand scene of confusion such as Alps or Himalayas cannot approach. I first resolved to turn towards the south, to the great ring of Clavius,—almost as large as Wales, with peaks as lofty as the Andes, and with ninety craters in its vast expanse,—about as many volcanoes as suffice for the whole earth. I mounted its lofty rampart, and resting on the highest peak, as high as Chimborazo, *i.e.*, some 23,000 feet, contemplated the superb and yet most strange scene.

These ring-mountains of the moon are almost as large as countries on the earth, and Clavius was more like a Swiss canton than a crater. Vast forces had been here at work! Were they the huge convulsions that destroyed life on your satellite? If not, if life could have existed in these lunar rings, each of them would be a separate country, as separated from the others as France is from Spain or Italy. Such ridges could not easily be passed by any but flying animals; but flying animals and a dense atmosphere probably never existed on the moon. If ever life existed on that world, it must have been very varied in its developments.

I dwelt on these thoughts as I rested upon the topmost peak of Clavius. I stayed there as long as one of your earth-days, and watched the shadows deepening on the cliffs. Then I thought of the bitter dreariness of the long night in this dead world; and before the shadows had lengthened on the craters I flew northward towards the equator.

I set forward my ether car and made for the twin rings (each as large as an English county) which men call Stoefler and Maurolycus. I thus again returned into the realm of Tycho, for two of his great rays came from his vast crater to Stoefler. These two ring-systems were in themselves most wonderful. Maurolycus with its ramparts as lofty as the Andes, and Stoefler as the Alps. Here, on one of the peaks between the two vast rings, I rested and looked for a while on the terrible desolation around me. A thousand peaks were in sight, chain beyond chain, ridge beyond ridge, of mountains;—the vast, glittering region of the lunar South Pole on the one side, and to the north the huge crater-chain rising in successive lines. " Is all this," I thought, " the result of the terrific convulsions that ruined life upon this satellite, or is it but the nature of this world—a world of mountain ranges,—of huge craters,—of volcanic action ?"

Then I rose upwards into the dark airless expanse of ether, and directed my car to the mighty ring of Ptolomæus.

CHAPTER II.

COPERNICUS.

FROM Ptolomæus I directed my car to the great ring of Copernicus, the rival of mighty Tycho. It was a vast plain of 56 miles diameter, walled in by ramparts, in rising terraces up to 12,000 feet. The peaks in succession glistened in the sunlight.

Then I turned westward from Copernicus to the huge chains of the lunar Apennines, which recalled to my mind, more than anything else I had seen since I had left Trehyndra, the memory of the mountains of the earth. Long lines of peaks with narrow gorges, with lines of awful precipices, such as you cannot imagine. Some of the peaks were as lofty as Mont Blanc. The scenery was magnificent and terrible.

From these peaks (on which I rested) I looked over the vast plains—those waterless seas of the moon—like what your Atlantic, or Pacific, or even North Sea, would be if the ocean was drained from them and only the sea-bottom left.

*   *   *   *

The feeling of loneliness intensified and grew rapidly upon me as the dark shadows of these tremendous peaks in the setting sun, sharply defined in the absence of an atmosphere, gathered around me. The valleys long had been in darkness. Now peak after peak grew black; at last night closed around me, and the bright orb of day sank amid the mountains.

The black sky was now varied by a myriad glittering stars, amid which the great earth rolled with its oceans and continents partly defined through the clouds and mist, with which, in many places, it was enveloped. I looked for England, but I only saw the mist in which it was wrapt. Some parts of the earth, however, came out clearly, especially the regions of the tropics. At either pole, just as you see on Mars, there was a glittering mass of snow and ice shining white in the sunlight.

I looked and wondered, and then I turned to the desolate scene around me, dimly illumined by the earth-light, and then, as I felt my loneliness—alone, alone, in a dead world,—I knelt in awe and worshipped God.

CHAPTER III.

WELCOME HOME.

I FINISHED the first prayer that for ages, perchance, had arisen from that dead world, and then I set my ether car homewards, and plunged out again into vast and boundless space, not to earth, but to our bright world.

At length, when some time had elapsed, such as men would count by weeks or months, our glorious world opened to my view, with its soft tints, and white, misty clouds, lighted by the sun's blaze,—and, here and there, the long ridges or the lofty peaks of the mountains.

As I drew nearer it, thoughts of home gathered around me. "Why 'had I left a world so lovely and so happy to dwell, even for a while, on one so fallen and so sad as earth is, or so utterly dead as its lifeless satellite,—the twin homes of sin and death? Yet, on the other hand, I had succeeded in my enterprise, and entirely so. I had visited earth, I had seen all its beauties and its sorrows; I had mixed with men, and been undetected by them; I had added immensely, not merely to my own, but to my fellow-creatures' field of knowledge. Now they would be able to classify and criticise my information, and by it advance in their grasp of the knowledge of creation."

Such thoughts passed through my mind as I directed my vessel through space to my own city, near the great Southern Ocean. Then I turned on the gravitating power, and dashed, at the speed of a cannon-ball, towards the glorious and brilliant globe before me. Down, down I rushed, till the sea of vapour was close under my feet. It reminded me then of the scene I more than once had lingered over in the Alps. The white sea of mist stretched before me, with here and there, like islands in a lake, a few of the glittering mountains of our South Polar continent. "After all, the solar system is really akin," I said to myself. "Surely our world is like to the earth, its sister in space."

Down, down I rushed. The clouds were round me, one sea of white mist; and then I had dashed through the veil, and our glorious, our lovely world, the "queen of beauty" in the solar system, opened to my view. There all was just as I had left it. There were the tall mountain-cliffs, huger far than the Himalayas, piercing up through the clouds into space; there were the soft, tinted forests, and the grey ocean, and the vast gardens of every delicate and tender hue. "How could I leave such a world to be on the earth, with all its misery and sadness?" I cried. "And yet the earth has its beauty, its loveliness. The gaily-coloured islands of the tropics, the green summer verdure of England, the virgin forests of America, have their beauties; for God has made all things good, even on earth." So thought I as I sped on my way. There was our city, with its many hundred towers and hanging gardens, and its thousand fantastic roofs. It was my home! Home, even if poor, on earth is beloved; but who would not be proud of such a home, seeing its grandeur now, as, for a year or more, I had only looked on earthly cities? Some had reminded me feebly of my fair home; for instance, Prague, with its mingled eastern and western architecture, and Edinburgh, and, in some sense, Paris.

I made first for the overhanging mountain, and there rested my car on a ledge, and

then, leaving it there in a quiet spot, flew over
the city. As in duty bound, I made first for
the temple of my ward (for we have seven
wards and seven great temples in our city).
Its lovely towers looked vast indeed by
contrast with anything I had seen on earth,
and when I flew through the great circular
door (like a rose window in the western gable),
how glorious it appeared! I had of late seen
Cologne Cathedral and St. Peter's at Rome,
and York and Durham. How poor they all
seemed in comparison with the church of our
ward! There are three things in which we
have an immeasurable advantage over men.
We have immortality, for the powers of death
have been conquered in us for ages, and so we
need not waste our powers in the struggle how
to live. We have had perfect peace, without a
possibility of war, for thousands of years. We
have a devotion to offer the vast resources in
our power to the service of religion. So the
poorest church of the smallest and most insig-
nificant city in our world is grander than the
finest cathedral or palace upon earth. Our
powers are immeasurably vaster than those of
man. Yet you might do much if you had no
war, and were to concentrate your powers on
the arts of peace.

As I entered, the service, of course, was going on: it has not ceased for ages. Four choirs of winged choristers were raising their pæans of joy and thankfulness. Night and day the song is unceasing. As I rested on the capital of a pillar and looked on the four choirs, in their robes of blue and red, green and purple, and heard the heavenly sound of many voices rolling through the lofty arches, soft and sweet and entrancing—now one choir, now another, now two combined, now all four together in one great chorus—I felt enthralled as I never felt before. "How wonderful is our world; how thankful am I to God for his love in placing me here!" So saying, I sank down gently on the pavement, and prostrated myself, adoring. None seemed to heed me, though many saw and knew me. The worship went on, and the delicious song still swept over me, and through the aisles and vaults, until the time when the thunder-signal marked the change in the course, and four other choirs, with solemn music, entered their places to continue the next watch of ceaseless adoration. Then I arose, and, going out with the choir, as I reached the garden, was met by many kindly greetings.

"Dear brother, we are glad to see you home

and happy. Tell us of the earth," was said by many of my comrades.

" Let me go to the prince of the ward, and then I shall tell you all. I have a thousand things to say, only I know not how to begin. Only now I shall say how much I love my home, and how glad you all should be of dwelling where you are."

So saying, followed by a friendly crowd, with many loving greetings, I came to the palace of the ward. Here, in the outer court, sat our prince upon his crystal throne, ready to welcome me, for many had seen me flying over the city, but none had spoken to me till I had finished my worship of the Most High.

"Welcome, Aleriel, he said, home ! God has preserved you in a long and perilous voyage, such as none, save the princes of the sun and the great spirit-messengers of the Highest, have yet taken. Welcome, tell us of your journey ! "

" I have so many thoughts, I know not how to tell them. It is a sad, a sorrowful world, that ' beautiful planet of the single satellite,' our twin sister in space. There is sin there, and death, and suffering, and disease, and war. I have seen all—all—much that is sad and terrible, such as we never even think of in our happy world. And yet it is beautiful. What God has made is beautiful, and that world is beautiful; not quite as lovely as ours, yet very lovely sometimes, and it is larger than ours; it has greater oceans and vaster continents. It is in some way fitted for happiness, and perhaps there is a something nobler and grander in man than in us; but in his earth-life man has no hope of perfect happiness, though on earth he is often fitted for perfect happiness in another life, when the penalty of sin has been paid, and Redemption been accepted."

"We ought, Aleriel, to be thankful to the Most High that we have been placed here, and not on that beautiful planet, our sister world in creation. It seems you have seen much sorrow and evil that you never would have known of had you not ventured over the abyss of space."

At my request, the prince sent for my car from its mountain ledge. It was soon brought down to me, and placed in the palace hall. Here I opened the larger case in which I had placed the packets of my earth-curiosities.

First and chief there were closely packed some thousands of photographs of earth's chief cities, and scenes from almost every land. This alone would have given months of study. But I had other things—some earth-flowers, pressed and dried, a phial of ocean and of fresh water for our naturalists to study; a pocket Bible, several specimens of earth's rocks, a few coins of different states, some pieces of polished woods. No animal or even insect could have lived in the airless realms of ether through which I had passed, so all I brought was dead—dead as the meteoric stones, the sole link in matter between the earth and other systems in space. Living beings only of the highest order and the most vigorous vitality can pass from world to world and live. So nothing earthly could exist even a hundred miles away from its own orb—man is a prisoner to his world.

These curiosities excited much attention and interest. Thousands were the questions I had to answer. Everything was examined, not merely with the naked eye, but with the microscopes that most of our citizens are wont to carry with them to investigate and admire any of the beauties of nature that attract their attention. Small shreds of many of the substances were taken by our chemists for analysis, to be quite sure that the elements of matter in our sister-world would be exactly the same as we had in our planet.

At once the news spread by electricity all over our world, and strangers from many far-off cities came to converse with me, and to see the earth-specimens I had brought. It was, indeed, with us just as it would be with you, if any one from another planet had come to earth with curiosities belonging to that distant world; what an excitement there would be in every intelligent society, in every city, in every university, at every observatory! But, alas, what wrangling would ensue! Not so with us. All knew I spoke only the truth, and that these things were really the product of our sister-world—the earth.

CHAPTER IV.

EARTH AS OTHERS SEE IT.

IT was a solemn yet a sublime moment when
I was called on to address the wisest and
noblest of the inhabitants of our world, and
tell them of my visit to the earth. The
assembly was vast, millions were gathered
along the ledges of the cliffs, and on the
slopes, and on the lower plain of the ring crater
wherein the assembly was gathered. I stood
by the prince of our city and sundry of the
great leaders of our nation, upon the central
platform, where, amidst the insignia of our
cities, I looked down on the gathered host.
Around me were the rings of microphones and
telephones to carry my voice to the uttermost
circle of that multitude. The host, with all
their robes of varied tints, made a gorgeous
spectacle, while the grand natural scenery of the
crater and its many cliffs was adorned in every
part by banners and insignia. I had never seen
such a spectacle since the Prince of the Sun

came with his message to us. When the assembly gathered, the signal was given, by the sound of cannon, for the opening hymn (for every national or general assembly was commenced by a tribute of praise to the Most High). Then from a million voices burst the long and mighty pæan of praise, with the soft music of ten thousand harps and trumpets. My spirit was moved to its depths as I looked down on the vast host before me, and thought of God's love to me in giving me so bright and glorious a world to live in. What a contrast to the earth—torn by strife, desolated by sin, stained by sorrow, suffering, misery! What a still greater contrast to the miserable dead world I had just left!

Then, as the majestic song of a million voices died away, the prince of our nation arose and waved his sceptre, and bade silence, and all was still as though no living being were in that huge crater. Then he spake:—

" Citizens of the bright world, listen! Aleriel, our brother, has come back from earth by divine permission. The awful journey through space has been achieved. Our prayers have been heard. Welcome him home."

He spake, and then from a million voices came the chanted song: " Aleriel, welcome home." I cannot tell you the thrill of that loving welcome. You cannot understand it now; but yet you may in a future state know the sweet welcome to a realm of bliss by angel voices.

Then he said aloud that all might hear :—

" Aleriel, tell us of your journey."

I was moved in spirit, and yet I rose and spoke.

" Thanks, comrades of a happy land. Be grateful for God's love to you. The story of my journey is very long, for I have seen so many million things which you hardly know of, for to me they were unknown until I saw them. I have been in that strange planet that so often lightens our evenings, when we see the outer skies through openings in the silvery mists. I have seen it; I have walked on it; I have twice travelled round it; I have visited its cities, traversed its oceans, crossed its continents, ascended its mountains. Man I have seen also—the ruling intelligence of that world. I have beheld man in his various races, in his struggles for higher things, in his sorrows, in his agonies, in his death. I have seen some noble things on earth, very many wretched and miserable things ; not a few, very terrible—to us inconceivably terrible. I have beheld men struggling against their misery, and in vain; I have witnessed starvation, want, disease in a thousand loathsome forms of death. I have seen the wretched selfishness of men grasping for self only; the weak crushed by the strong, and the strong still insatiate. It is a world in which there are many terrible, and horrible, and despicable things, and a few noble or glorious. Yet, as to the world itself, it is, like all God's work, good of itself. Nature on earth is often very beautiful. In some things it rivals in loveliness our world. In the evenings often the silvery light of the satellite gives it a mysterious and soft beauty, such as we have not, and by day even many a scene is grand and brilliant. That green gem-like island south of the great continent* is very beautiful, and so in colder regions are many parts of the fair isles west of the great continent. The regions round the equator are full of splendid scenes. Even colder realms, in their frequent changes, have great variety—some silvery in whiteness, when the moist rain falls frozen to the earth in flakes; or in spring, green; or in summer, of many hues, growing more sober as winter comes. The

* Ceylon.

oceans are grand also, and the storms, when the blue waters are silvered with foam. Yes, God made all things good—even on earth. It is only man that makes them vile. How strange it seems that bond of man to evil—that clinging to the bad, even of those who wish to be good and to love the good! It seems like an evil nature, a secret spiritual power, marring God's creation on earth, which over us has never had any influence. Yet men who conquer this evil, how noble they grow, how majestic in spirit! The very struggle makes them nobler, stronger in spirit, grander even than we are. Such souls as good men have are fitted for a higher existence, not only than earth, but even than our lovely world can offer. Our natures are soft, and gentle, and simple; but we have never known the struggle against sin and sorrow that men know.

"I have seen many things that you never can see on our world. I have seen the hospital—men and women struggling with death in dying agony. I have seen misery such as you cannot fancy—thousands, tens of thousands, without enough of light or air, in smoky, dingy, dirty dens, lingering on a weary life to make others rich. I have seen debauchery and sins, such as we have, happily, no name for. I have seen wickedness triumphant, proud, rich, self-sufficient; and I have seen men and women struggling almost against hope—save that one blessed anchor of the human soul, the expectation of a joyful resurrection. I have seen untold misery such as you cannot conceive, and I have seen what is far worse than misery, human souls carried on to ruin by the mad thirst for pleasure. O sad earth! beautiful and glorious though thy God has made thee! what an untold depth of woe is to be seen on thy fair lands!"

The vast assembly seemed moved to sorrow by my words; a sympathetic thrill went through them. I noticed it and changed the subject, struck at how much my fellow-beings felt for and pitied men who were not as happy as they were.

" In that world the forms of life akin to our lower nature are humble, small, weak, stupid, soulless. The earth cannot develope the flying type of life to a great size or intelligence. The beings akin to us are smaller than men, and of low sense; as the beings akin to man (*i.e.* the creatures who climb the trees) are in our world feeble and despised. The mountains of earth are not as ours. Even the Himalayas and the Alps—those white spots you see on the great continent—are mere hills compared with the ring mountains of our world. Man cannot even yet fly, but sometimes as a great feat he risks his earth-life by floating on a huge gas ball in the air, carried by every current. All on earth clings to the surface, and ever has so clung. Even in the ages long gone by before the days of man, the huge beings of primeval time crawled in the marshes. Only a few birds soar a mile or so in the air, and those birds are thought wonderful, the ensigns and heraldic signs of earth's greatest monarchies. Earth is one vast prison-house, where all are bound to the surface.

"What the destiny of earth is to be I cannot say. Men, the most thoughtful and most holy of mankind, believe it is to be destroyed, to be wrapped in some vast cataclysm, and in the great crash of doom be ruined utterly and eternally. Better, methinks, it should be so. It has its work to do in training up brave souls to endure hardness, to develope in the spiritual combat their hidden nobleness. When that work is done and enough human souls have struggled, striven, conquered in the agony of that great combat, better that earth should pass away and be broken up and crushed in atoms, and then there will be an end to earth and to the earth-life of man, and the strong souls that once were men in the higher life of other worlds will glory in their victory. For their souls are immortal, and, if they cannot obtain their destiny on earth, they will in higher and happier spheres."

CHAPTER V.

A STRANGE PROPOSAL.

I CAME home to my city. I rested there a quarter of a year (we have no months, because we have no moon). Many came from distant cities to ask about earth and what I had seen or heard. Myriads of questions were put to me—some that I could, and many that I could not, answer.

The pictures of earth—your cities, mountains, river scenes and so on—were examined by myriads of our comrades, copied again and again, and copies sent to every city and every museum of our world. My journey was given in writing, and ten million copies scattered through every country. Many were the comments on it. Some even foolishly suggested that a party of our citizens should go forth as missionaries to your world to teach men to be better and happier; but I at once checked this idea. " The Church on earth does her work," I said, "and God deals with men in His way.

Our going openly to men would only make them worse—might disturb the good and form a mere pastime to the wicked." So the wise ones of our world stifled the proposal in its germ.

One evening, as I was returning from the service of our course in the great temple of the city, I found our prince waiting for me in my home. With him there was a stranger, who, by his robes and insignia, I recognised must be one of the princes of Saldonio, the city of the stars, in our northern continent, where the study of astronomy was chiefly carried on, more than anywhere else. "I have long read and re-read the narration of your visit to the earth," he said, "and it has filled me with interest. It seems to me that the time has come when we may, by subduing the forces of nature, travel from world to world; not only to the earth, but to the farther worlds of our system. Our mechanician, Azoniel, has constructed a globe fitted for such journeys, and has perfected your mode of conquering gravitation. My friend Ezariel, one of the leading masters of the laws of nature in our city, will join us."

I gave reflection to the proposal. At first the love of home, stronger than ever since I

had seen earth's miseries and sorrows, made
me unwilling again to launch forth into immeasurable space; but I was unwilling to deny
myself the pleasure of beholding new works of
the Creator's love, new evidences of His mercy
and His majesty, and also I reasoned that, perchance, other worlds might be as beautiful as
earth, but less fallen and spoilt by sin. So,
perchance, in other worlds I might behold
better and fairer things, by which I might learn
more. I consulted with the chief sages of our
city. They were of opinion that now I had
been able to pass to two of our sister orbs, it
would be well to try if we could proceed further.
Some suggested Mercury as suitable for a trial;
but my own feeling, and that of the great
majority of our senate, was that, if we should
again plunge forth into space, we should select
the outer worlds rather than the inner planet
of our system. The gorgeous realm of Mars,
and even the huge systems of the giant and
the ringed worlds (as we call Jupiter and
Saturn) might be visited.

I went to Saldonio in our air car. It was a
long journey of three days, half round our
world, for Saldonio was in a far-off continent.
Thousands of fair cities, vast territories of
beauteous vegetation, lakes, rivers, and seas did

we pass over, night and day. Still on we flew, until, at last, we reached the mighty mountain ring, upon one peak of which Saldonio was reared. It was built on a plateau of rock some twenty miles above the plains, far above the fleecy clouds which usually cover our planet. Thus the astronomers could usually watch in clear nights the expanse of heaven, and all the wonders therein contained. Around the city, from many miles afar, were to be seen the lower mountains of the chain rounded into the form of spheres, each of which depicted some world in the solar system, carved over and stained as gigantic models of the planets around us. Close to the city was the model of the earth, a globe far vaster than any man has ever made, six hundred yards around, on which the loftier Himalayas were raised some four or five inches, and where London was marked as a dark spot about the size of a large leaf.

I came to the city over which enormous instruments of study towered above every spire and roof. It was a wondrous place. All that art could do was done to know the other worlds. They were observed, mapped, examined, measured. Science had done everything, save open the gates to visiting them. And now Arauniel was planning that also.

He welcomed me in the Palace of the Stars. He showed me the treasures of the city—the results of the studies of thousands of astronomers for many ages past, and inspired me with his interest and curiosity to know more. At last he showed me, in Azoniel's hall (where his works of mechanism were stored) the globe for a voyage through space. It was a sphere of some twenty feet diameter, of strongest polished steel. At its top there was a rounded door which could be lifted up, and around its equator were four crystal windows, to observe as we travelled through space. Within were copies of my instruments for conquering gravitation, but of enormous power. Mighty electromagnets were there, and within there was a room with every comfort for the travellers during their long and perilous voyage. In the side were a thousand instruments of every kind for observing, measuring, registering natural forces, and so forth. A long bar pierced the base of the sphere in which were the explosive forces to impel or direct the sphere. It was a wonderful triumph of skill—a little artificial world, as it were, fitted to dart through interplanetary space with every triumph of our skill and science comprised within its globe and stored in its many cells. All accidents appeared provided against, while the apparatus gave us an immense power over nature.

I admired the ether car, as we called it, and felt inclined to join once more in a great expedition into space beyond the earth's orbit, and into the vast outer regions of the giant planets.

I returned from Saldonio to our city, calling, as I went on, at most of the great cities on the way, and studying, in their museums, both of the things which might relate to earth and also to my coming voyage. I talked with the wisest sages of many lands on our project, and on the things we might hope to see, and what should be the special points of our researches. I found the general opinion was that life was universal in the solar system, except in some few of the smaller worlds (like the moon) on which it had existed, but had passed away, or which were, as yet, not enough developed to receive it. The idea was that, as in the spectroscope we had seen that the elements of the solar system were everywhere the same as on our world, probably derived from the sun—and, as on your earth, only the same metals and gases were proved to exist as we had—so also, in life, that the same types of life were everywhere existent, only developed more in

one world than in another. I satisfactorily
had proved that, as the metals and the common forces, so the life-types were the same in
your world as in ours ; so, also, we hoped to
find whether they could be traced all through
the solar system, just as the metals were
traced.

PART III.—MARS.

CHAPTER I.

THE VOYAGE THROUGH SPACE.

AT length the day appointed for our depar-
ture arrived. We had resolved to start
from Saldonio. The ether-car was fixed to the
central spire of the chief cathedral of the city—
one of the highest points of our world. About
two millions of our Venusians had gathered to
behold the spectacle, and now they crowded
every vantage point in the city—every spire
and tower, every battlement and roof, every
square and garden, was thronged with the vast
host who had gathered from all lands to behold
the sight. Their variously coloured robes and
ornaments formed a most brilliant scene.

It was about sunset. After the tranquil
service in the glorious cathedral, and the
solemn blessing of the chief priests of the city,

H

we passed forth into the crowded square, and flew up to the spire where the ether-car was suspended. A sublime spectacle (such as I have never seen in all my wanderings excelled) opened to our vision. At our feet for a hundred miles or more stretched the vast Saldonian territory, the lines of mountain chains and rings, and forest-clad hills, and milky lakes. The shadows of evening were already gathering over the low country, for Saldonio was so lofty that it was in sunlight when the evening had wrapt the plains. The lights of a hundred cities were just glimmering in the grey evening. At our feet was the magnificent city—a city such as you cannot imagine (though Edinburgh might be mentioned as a feeble parody of it), with its thousands of graceful spires, and airy gardens and plazas and public buildings—now one living mass of intelligent beings, in their varied coloured robes. It was a scene not to be described in human words.

We entered the ether-car. The chiefs of the city bade us farewell, and gave us their blessing. At a signal from the Prince of Saldonio, the great hymn of praise burst from two millions of voices, and just as the sun sank behind the serrated ridge of the Ulcorian mountains we cut the bond, developed the anti-gravitating force, and launched into infinite space.

*   *   *   *

I need not describe the long journey into interplanetary space we took. We soon reached one of the meteoric systems which traverse ether in all directions, and swept on by it towards the planet Mars. What you call days and weeks and months passed as we rushed on away and away from the great Sun.

The time did not pass as heavily, however, as I found it on my former lonely journey. Companionship brightens life even to us, more perhaps than to men, for we Venusians have never anything unkind to say, no quarrel, no bitterness, no selfishness, no pride, no envy to trouble each other with. So we talked, or studied the precious books that Arauniel had stored us with, or compared notes and conjectures what we should see in those other worlds which we should visit.

At length we passed the earth's orbit, but at many millions of miles from the earth, and then went on, further and further, into space, till the ruddy orb of Mars grew larger, and then we severed ourselves from the meteors and restored gravitation and dashed át immense velocity to that gorgeous world.

CHAPTER II.

THE ICE ISLAND.

OUR descent was planned for the Great Ice Island in the Delarue Ocean. It was a bright spot from our world, and so we had chosen it as one suited for a first descent—the more as it seemed isolated, and probably our arrangements would not be disturbed.

On then we flew through space till we reached the attraction of the ruddy planet, and could see his mighty expanse of crimson plains spotted by green oceans and lakes and veiled in clouds with either pole robed in eternal snows. It was autumn in the Southern hemisphere of Mars then, and the white glittering snows stretched over the south. But Huyghens continent and even Laplace land, ruddy with their mighty forests, glowed blood-stained, as it were, beneath us.

On, on we rushed, ever faster and faster, by the power of gravitation of the world to which we were approaching. How vast it seemed;

and yet, as we all know, it is smaller far than either your world or than ours. At length the whole expanse beneath us, the equatorial region of Mars, was red or green. Then the ruddy shores of Copernicus and Galileo continents only were in sight on the horizon, with the two great islands which earth's astronomers call Tycho's Island and Schroeter's Land. All else was the green ocean absorbing the sun's rays into its dark emerald verdure. On we flew to the crystal peaks covered with snows of the great Ice Island. They were huge mountains, not unlike your Alpine group of Mont Blanc and Monte Rosa. A vast region of snowy peaks glittering in the Sun, but unlike Switzerland, not set in green, heaving lands, but in the storm-toss'd waves of the Delarue Ocean —like the peak of Teneriffe in the Atlantic.

Down we sank until at last the anti-gravitating power had to be used to stem the impetus, and even when we reached the snowy peak of one of the ice mountains, we struck it with a violence that almost cracked the rock. Our vessel was, however, strongly constructed, and so it was merely shaken.

Again I felt the joy of treading the firm ground of another world. This was the fourth I had stood upon. My native world had even for ages been my joy—a happy abode. Earth I had trodden on and traversed, even in places where man's foot had never wandered, in Arctic snows, up to the very Pole itself.   I had twice gone round your earth, had seen its cities, mountains, oceans, its sin, its misery, its follies, its conceits. Your satellite I had visited and wandered, as I told you, over the rugged slopes of Tycho, and clambered the lunar crater range, and crossed the crater of Copernicus.

And now I stood upon another world—a world that seemed most beautiful, although further removed than ours or yours from the great source of life and beauty, *i.e.*, the glorious centre of our system—the light-giving Sun.

We found ourselves on the summit of a small ice-formed mountain, partially filled with snow. Here we placed our ether-car and buried it in the snows, so that it might not be disturbed by any Martian who might come across it. Then we took flight to the loftiest peak of the ring, from which we surveyed the country.

In the foreground of the strange scene before us was a vast succession of mountains, not unlike icebergs, or the lunar mountains of the South pole. They were all white with snow, or glittering here and there with icy glaciers. The scene reminded me of some parts of the Moon, and of the lofty plateau of the Dofrefeld. But beyond it and below, was neither lunar desolation nor brown plains of moorland, nor green fields and forests as in your European snowy mountain ranges. As the snows were lost in the low country, vast forests appeared—crimson as blood, or orange-coloured—glowing in the sunlight with a rich deep red. They grew on the ledges of the cliffs under the snows, on the mountain terraces, and lastly stretched down in slopes to the green waters of the Delarue Ocean.

We resolved to plunge downwards to these forests. We flew easily to one of the terraces with overhanging cliffs around it. Here we alighted amidst this crimson vegetation. The effect, as the sun shone through the blood-red leaves, was unutterably superb. The very light was tinted to a ruddy glow. All was gorgeous and magnificent. There is a certain majesty and power in the colour of red which, when seen in large fields, impresses the mind. But no one who has not seen vast masses of red all around in every direction above (in leafy foliage), below in the ruddy, as it were, blood-stained turf, around—in vegetation of quaint forms, but of crimson hue, can realise the inexpressible gorgeousness of this spectacle— a field of peonies or other red flowers would very feebly represent it, for these red flowers of earth have green leaves, and ours have pale and delicate tints; but all was here, as it were, ensanguined in hue. To men's eyes the sight would soon have been wearying, or even maddening; to us it was simply magnificent.

It would not be fair, however, to say that only red was present. It is true, the very light was tinted with red as it passed through the ruddy vegetation; but there were other tints besides, and glorious ones, but only enough to vary the spectacle and to make it splendid. Every colour of the rainbow was there, but crimson and orange predominated. Every other colour was, as it were, set in a glorious back-ground of red. The forms of the plants, for such I suppose I must call them, were various—very different from ours or yours,— quaint growths in curious developments of form, yet not without a certain grace and elegance, for all that God has made is good.

We walked a little while among these strange productions of nature in all their ruddiness, when I heard a rolling sound, and calling the attention of my companions, we walked to-

wards it among the quaint cactus-like plants
and trees that made up this wondrous forest.
At length we saw something green glittering
amidst the red foliage. We came nearer to it.
Then we saw the cause of the sound; it was
the cascade of green liquid that flowed down
with crash and noise from the terrace above.
Here, then, were the causes of the Martian
tints—*i.e.*, the green waters and the ruddy
foliage of that which men once called the war
planet; not the mere red rocks (like your
Devonian red sand-stone on earth), but that
which everywhere results from moisture and
sunlight and warmth — vegetation and vegetable life. This ruddy foliage is not unknown
to you. The copper-beech is a slight approach
to it, the poppy, and the peony, and the red
geranium are better examples though on a
minute scale. And even green is not unknown
in earth seas. I have seen it often when the
sun has shone through blue seas on yellow
sands—so Mars is not so unearth-like as many
planets are.

The Ice Island seemed to be a vast mass of
icebergs that had attached themselves to an
island covered with vegetation. We resolved
at once to leave it for Tycho Island.

CHAPTER III.

TYCHO ISLAND.

ON we flew over the green Delarue Ocean, till at length the white peaks of the ice mountains were lost behind the waves. Soon a blood-red line appeared on the horizon. It grew clearer and clearer. The shores were more and more defined. Then there opened up the long red forests of Tycho Island—the great island of Mars—the largest tract of land enclosed in the green ocean of the southern tropics. It was very glorious and gorgeous. The red forests waved like gigantic poppies or carnations in the breeze. We floated over them. Everything looked unlike what we all had seen on our own fair world, or I on earth. The tints were not the soft pale tints of our sunny home, nor yet the refreshing green or dull browns of the earth, but glowing gorgeous red and orange. The shapes of the trees were such as I cannot describe—quaint and extraordinary—a new phase of creation, and, to us, fresh manifestations of creative power and love. Glorious in form, as in colour, were those ruddy forests of Mars. As yet we could see no trace of intelligent beings; but, after floating in the air for some hours, Ezariel said: "See, there is something like the abode of an intelligence, or of something possessing reason."

It was a massive wall of grey stone in a triangular form under some large red trees. Upon it there was a metal roof, which glittered in the sunlight. This roof was conical in form, and quaintly ornamented. We approached it, and passed by a path through the ruddy cactus-shaped plants. The building looked one constructed to resist pressure from without—massive and strong.

"Surely," said Ezariel, "this must be formed to resist outward pressure, and cast off the winter snows. This is an Arctic clime. The winters must be terrible, and so it would appear the first object of the Martians must be to keep off the snow, and to exclude the cold."

Under the forest shade, as we descended, we saw a figure half human in aspect—erect and dignified—but gigantic in figure. His face was very like a man's and like ourselves, but yet he had a sort of lion look also in his limbs.

We approached him. For a moment he seemed awed and alarmed by us—the natural shrinking of every living being from the creature of another world was manifest on our side and on his. Yet we felt no antipathy. There was a nobleness and a dignity in his presence which, though distinct from the soft lovingness of our nature, was not opposed to it. His manner was rather of astonishment than of fear. He looked at us in silence for a while, and then as we halted at some distance he himself approached us, and waved his hand in the air, keeping still erect, as if in greeting. We made the signs of greeting and sang, as is our wont, the song of welcome to a friend. He listened, as if moved and enthralled, then in deep solemn tones, from his great chest, heaved out some words that we could not understand.

"It seems that where there is intelligence there is speech," said Ezariel. "Perhaps it always follows the gift of reason."

"We have found it so far," I said, "but we may not in other worlds. It seems here reason implies speech."

We followed him towards the house to which he beckoned us. He came to it and touched a boss in the outer wall. A portcullis arose at once, and left an opening. He beckoned to us to enter. We followed him into a domed hall, deeply and closely padded with thick fur-like substances. The door was shaped somewhat like an opening flower, and so were the windows, which were deeply and richly coloured in divers hues. In the centre was a low metal pillar (apparently of brass) supporting a large plate. On this, directly he entered, our guide lighted a fire, over which he made sundry signs and gestures towards us.

"Surely," said Ezariel, "this is their mode of greeting. All seems adapted against cold, and perhaps the lighting of this fire is a symbol of welcome. Let us imitate him."

We did so, and also made signs of greeting close by the fire. He then opened another small door close by, and presently brought with him another Martian, differently attired, but also having a long flowing fur-like robe, with a still greater number of metallic ornaments. Her look was softer and gentler than her dignified husband, and she evidently feared us more—indeed, she shrank back when she saw us; but after some delay she also came to the fire and made signs over it like her husband.

She then retired, and soon brought to us a

crystal vase full of fruits. She held them over the fire, and rather timidly presented them to us warm. They were grateful to eat—warm and aromatic.

"You see, still," said Ezariel, "the fire symbol prevails. They welcome us by warmth. It is evident that in this world cold is counted the greatest of evils."

After we had partaken of the food, we had a short consultation as to what we had better do, Ezariel proposed that he and Arauniel should remain in retirement in that quiet forest district, or in the Ice Island, while I, profiting by my experience on earth, should endeavour to acquire the Martian language, and go among the people. Strange to say, both my companions expressed a great shrinking from the Martians, and as it was understood we were to keep a rigid incognito, we agreed that it was better for me to travel alone, while they studied the almost infinite natural treasures around them.

A venerable and majestic-looking Martian suddenly entered as we were discussing our projects. He was as tall as his comrade, *i.e.*, some nine feet high, but grave and apparently aged. His face was thoughtful, and he had an appearance of authority. Around his neck there hung a large chain, and a silver symbol of two triangles. On the chain I traced some of the well-known letters of the alphabet of the heavens. This cheered me. I at once saw that here was one with whom there might be a basis of communication. After greeting us, which he did solemnly, and with gestures evidently of a religious character, he seemed to welcome us as fellow-creatures called into being by the same Creator.

The thought struck me of a mode of communication. I drew from my vest a tablet, and wrote on it symbols in our hieroglyphic character expressing where I came from. With a little difficulty and some gesticulation, I made him understand our symbols, which expressed the sentence, "We, Aleriel, Arauniel, and Ezariel, come in the ether ship from the beautiful planet near the sun." When he understood what I had written, he said something to the other Martian, who expressed great astonishment and wonder. Then, having paused awhile, as if in thought, he drew from the fold of his robe a box, whence he took a sheet of a cloth-like texture, on which he traced in large and rude characters, in a system of celestial picture-writing, not the same as ours, but sufficiently like it to be intelligible to us:

" Welcome to this our Martian world. Do not reveal who you are, or that you come from the planet near the sun, in the name of God."

This confirmed our resolution to keep our *incognito*. It was evident that there would be danger to others, if not to ourselves, if our nature was revealed. So I symbolised assent, and so did my two comrades.

Then I wrote in hieroglyph, " I want to learn your Martian language." Here a difficulty arose, for their symbol for language was evidently different to ours. But by gesture I showed them what I meant, and he at once wrote :

" Come to my house and I will teach you."

He then made some signs to the female, who went out by another door, and soon returned with a robe much smaller than her own (which probably belonged to one of her children). She threw it around me, and drew a fur-like hood over my head.

Evening had now come in. The sunlight ceased to glow through the rich-toned colours of the stained windows. The clear sky was adorned by stars in the same constellations as you know so well—for the sidereal heavens are the same for all the solar system. The distance between us and Neptune is not enough to make serious displacement in a single constellation. There was the Southern Cross and Orion and Sirius, just as on the earth, all glistening in the darkness, and the ruddy trees were now a very dark crimson, or almost black in the more shady places.

We passed along a forest path, with many strange forms looming in the gloom. At length we reached a little hill, covered with rocks, under one of which, nestled in a corner, was a domed house such as we had left. My conductor ushered me in. There was a chamber like the other, adorned with many thousand symbols in picture-writing all over the walls and roof.

CHAPTER IV.

A MARTIAN INSTRUCTOR.

NEXT morning I commenced my study of the Martian language. The picture-writing was not difficult, for the symbols were the same in principle as ours, founded, indeed, on the bases of geometry, or natural symbolism, such as must be almost universal. The circle meant space, the point meant unity, the multiplication of points meant numbers, the equal lines meant equality, the crossed lines meant addition, the picture of the thing meant the thing depicted. It was the same symbolism as was the basis of human writing in the Egyptian hieroglyphic or the ancient Chinese, a small part of which still lingers with you in mathematical and masonic symbols. It was the language, not of a particular world, but of the universe; still it had local symbols for ideas belonging to that Martian world. These I had to learn, but my instructor soon put me in the way of them by explaining them through general symbols.

When I could read the Martian writing, I found there was another, as on earth, phonetic mode of writing, short and simple as your shorthand, which represented sounds, and was in common use. By this I was soon able to learn the spoken language, and thereby to converse with my instructor by word of mouth.

The spoken language was very simple. Each syllable conveyed an idea, the consonant sounds representing the idea in its special sense, the vowel sound the part of speech or grammatical inflection. Thus all roots were consonants, all inflexions vowel sounds. By this the idea was in the consonants, and the part of speech, the form of the idea, was in the vowels. Thus, supposing we were to adopt this system in England, *man* would represent the thought man, *m..n* meaning humanity, and *a* marking a noun *Mān* would be "men." *Men* would be "manly." *Min* "to man," or " provide with men." *Mon* "to be manly." *Mun* would be " manliness." And so the idea would be altered through some score of vowel sounds.

" Have you many languages in your world, as they have on earth?" I asked my instructor.

" We had them once, but we agreed to abolish

them, and substitute one as near perfection as we could make it. It is far better for a world to have only one language. Now, one can travel from land to land without hindrance, and converse with people of all nations. It is many centuries since we had diversity of speech."

" How did you arrange this ?"

" We had some ages ago a great congress on this subject, where all the assembly agreed to have one language. An academy was formed to establish a perfect language. After long discussion, a scheme was adopted and submitted to the whole world again, and accepted. This was taught in all the schools, and in time, as the young grew old and died off, the old languages died with them, or rather were reserved for a study of a few of the learned. Since then we have had but one language."

" It almost looks," I said, " as if on earth, as with you and us, this may in time be the case, for two quarters of the earth are accepting the use of one language—the English. Perhaps it may in time be dominant. But yours is a formed, not a natural language."

" Partly so ; but only in part, for we still retain the basis of the ancient tongues."

" Have you any exceptions in your language ?"

" No, none ; a rule once given is always preserved. In the old languages corruptions and exceptions did exist, in the new none."

As soon as we could thus converse together easily, my instructor asked me many thousands of questions about my world, and also (when he learnt I had been on Earth) about yours. He seemed of a most inquisitive mind, and anxious to learn all I could teach him about our worlds. It seemed that the first elements of astronomy were as well understood by him, as by your best astronomers. Observations had been systematically carried on for ages, and instruments had been perfected. The Martians evidently wished, as far as they could, mentally to soar above the little world to which they had been bound, and on which they lived. They had measured the distances of their sister worlds from their own, and from the mighty Sun ; they had examined their elements in the spectroscope, they had watched their movements.

I asked him once about the history of his world, and what was its past.

" There was a time," he said, " when war raged in our world most terribly. Each of our four great continents were separate nations. Each struggled for supremacy. Each strove

to obtain sovereignty over all the rest—a
sovereignty bought at a terrible price. All
countries were desolated; population was re-
duced to a hundredth. Many evil souls were
sent forth from our world unfitted for a higher
state. Then God looked on us with pity.
Our world was losing her use in this vast
creation, as the fitting abode of spirits for
awhile incarnated to prepare for a higher life
in happier spheres. Then, in His love, He
sent the Holy One to teach us better. He
taught us useful lessons, that peace, not war,
was the source of happiness; that love, not
hate, was the due of all; but the Holy One
taught us also to hate sin, and lying, falsehood,
and gross low pleasure. And our ancestors
learnt the lesson. We had been united by
force into one state, and now were taught to
love one another. Peace was established; but
still our sensitive, irritable natures were eager
to hate something. We were taught to hate
sin, and, if needed, to slay the sinner. A
great war arose then against Sin, and was
waged against all who erred against our pristine
nobleness; and so the law was instituted that
those who erred against truth, or honour, or
(in females) against modesty, should be cast
out of our world; but yet cast out lovingly, in

the hope that in another life they might do better. And so the arts of peace prospered among us. The energy wasted in war was given to science and to progress, to seek to know more, to draw forth nature's secrets, to develop, to ennoble our race, to increase the sum of happiness. And so we prospered. Cities were raised where only forests grew before. The wild beasts were tamed and utilized, knowledge was augmented, and the forces of nature were subdued to our will. Population increased wonderfully. There were millions where there had been hundreds. Still we sought to increase the means of subsistence, and nature wonderfully answered our demands. Our world began to assume its true position in creation."

"Tell me," I said, "what is your government? How do you secure peace?"

"In the olden days of wars and mutual destruction, as I said, we had four great states—four great nations—for our four continents, with minor states on the islands. All these contended against each other. But then, when the Holy One's teachings were established, and peace and love accepted, the first step was to give each of the four nations their rights. The great principle of unselfishness was established, and only those who excelled in wisdom and virtue were promoted to positions of trust and power."

" I should like much to see some of your great cities. May I not do so ? "

" Yes, I think you may—only disguise yourself. It would not be well for you to own yourself to be of another world than ours. It might put some of our weaker ones into temptation. Foolish curiosity would be excited; you would find much trouble for yourself and for us, so you must disguise yourself."

So he arranged a disguise for me as a child of the Martians, to cover my inferior size, and stained me to a colour like theirs, and otherwise disguised me so that I could hardly know myself.

So one day he took me out again into the forest, and told me that we should go together to the City of the Waters, the capital of the great island on which he dwelt. It was situated between the great Delarue Ocean, and that wide lake you call the Lockyer Sea, the point whence earth's astronomers usually calculate the meridians of the ruddy world.

As we walked on we conversed on many subjects.

" We are wont to travel much in this our

land," he said, "for our winters are very cold. In our early state, ages and ages ago, we Martians used to have but one home, and when the snow came and the cold, we used to huddle up ourselves in our houses and cause artificial heat, and so spend the wretched winter. Hence have arisen our fire customs. Now, as science has progressed, every one, except those who live near the equator, has two homes, one in the northern and the other in the southern hemisphere, and also most have an electric ship and car; so, when the winter comes on, the family enter their ship, and float down to the port of the other home with all their goods, and so it is with each commune. The same friends gather together in the other hemisphere as here, and all home comforts are the same, with the same friends, the same community in the southern as in the northern hemisphere. There, then, we dwell till again autumn comes, when we go back again all together to the old home to find spring once more. We thus live now in constant spring and summer."

"You are like the migratory birds, it seems, of earth, which never stay for winter. Possibly, in ages to come, men may be like this, when modes of transit improve. The rich sometimes already are so 'cheating the winter' in warm climes."

" From what you said about earth," said my conductor, " and the state of humanity there, I should say it was a world as yet far less developed than ours—perhaps younger in the scale of creation, a younger child of the glorious sun, and yet very like ours. Men appear, as yet, hindered by sin, wars, bad government, intestine quarrels, and class selfishness, from reaching the state in which we are. And yet, in our history, I can well trace a period, many thousands of years ago, when we Martians were no further advanced in enlightenment, or in the knowledge of what was best for ourselves, than you say you found mankind upon the earth during your recent visit. Perhaps the time may come, in thousands of years hence, when the human race may attain something like the state of society in which we Martians now live. The two worlds are very much alike in everything. In the future, perhaps, men who live in cold countries will usually quit them for summer climes."

We had not walked many minutes in the forest before, almost suddenly, his words about winter appeared realised. The sky was clouded over, the white snow fell on the ruddy vegetation. I cannot describe how lovely it appeared. Above, the leaves were glittering white and ornamented with exquisite snow crystals; but below, their ruddy glow was manifest.

" This snowfall is not unlike," I said to him, "what I have often seen in earth-winter in northern Europe. Really, if it were not for the ruddy foliage, this might almost be a scene upon the earth."

" Yes," he replied, " I was prepared for that remark. The two worlds are very much alike in almost everything—in snowfall, in summer sun and winter cold, in distribution of land and water into continents and seas, in islands and lakes. We even think we sometimes can trace a resemblance in the northern part of one of the hemispheres of earth to our world."

" You mean in North America, in Canada, and the lake regions of the United States. It is true the configuration of the country there is very like what we see in Mars."

Meanwhile, the snow fell more and more heavily. My guide led me to a shelter which had been formed by some rocks, and here we waited for the snow shower to pass.

" You were talking of your continents and islands with which your world is mapped out.

Tell me, how can I see them, and traverse your globe as I have done the earth? You advise me to maintain my secret, but I fear my disguise will not suffice me to do what I managed safely to do upon the earth. Our difference in size alone makes it impracticable."

" I think we can do it, but you must go with me. Listen to my proposal. When we reach the Ocean city, if you desire it, we may embark together on the little electric ship of our commune, which I have at my disposal. I can easily navigate her myself in every sea and port."

" Is it possible? Can one Martian alone, with a single companion, navigate a vessel round the whole of his world? No man has ever attempted such a feat yet. It is almost impossible."

" You forget," said my companion, " the conditions of the voyage are quite different to those which men would have to encounter on earth. Our oceans are not so vast, from shore to shore is not so far, our electric ships are exquisitely constructed to give a complete power over the natural forces; we have but to connect or to disjoin a wire to establish or destroy an immense force, and electricity is, as you know, the key force, the master force of our solar system. By my command of this power in my little vessel I can go anywhere on the waters, and do anything."

We reached a shed close to a railroad of polished steel. From the shed he drew an electric car, and mounting it, bade me do so likewise. He touched the electro-motor and we dashed through the forest.

CHAPTER V.

THE OCEAN CAPITAL.

AT length we came to a mountain-side, up which the electric engine crept, amidst rocks and cliffs and ruddy woodlands. On a sudden, by a turn of the road, a strange scene opened before my eyes, such as I shall strive, though ill able to describe it in earthly words, to depict. A vast plain lay before us, stretching towards the green sea of what you call the Delarue Ocean. Its surface was not all ruddy, but speckled with great white spots of shining metal, which glistened in the sun, and tall spires and towers varying the expanse. Over it there were extended various ramifications, like a spider's web, of hanging railroads in long lines, crossing and intersecting each other, resting on huge pillars and massive towers. It stretched for twenty miles away, or more, sinking into the horizon on one side, but, on the others, bounded by mountains and the green sea.

" Is that your Ocean capital of which you spoke ? " I asked.

" It is," he replied. " Here is the capital of the seas ; but we have several other cities great as this, and even still more beautiful. The capital of Learning you shall see in the great northern continent. The four capitals of the four continents are each as great as this."

" The greatest city I have yet seen," I said, " is on the earth. It also is an ocean capital in some sense ; the centre of the earth's trade. It has four millions of people in it. What is the population of this ? "

" Five millions and more."

" But they extend over a vast extent, far vaster than that great city on the earth."

" Perhaps so ; but you see we do not crowd our people. Each one of the twenty wards of this great city has its public park and gardens for the health and enjoyment of the citizens, to give them the contact of Nature even in the city, which is the right of every living creature. Every dwelling is isolated from the others, to avoid fire, and to give free ventilation. Every street is planted with trees. So the city extends over a huge extent, as you perceive. But, see ! we are passing its borders, the ancient fortifications reared in the days of war."

We came to a mighty wall, almost a little mountain ridge of rock, carved in quaint style, and flanked with triangular towers, on which still were placed curious engines of war, which appeared worn out by age and falling to pieces.

" They have left these as a memory of past times. We destroy nothing of the works of ancient days ; but they are mere curiosities now, useful to remind us of the errors of our ancestors, and to warn us to keep in better paths. How many thousands have been launched into eternity upon and before these walls ! But all is over now. War never can return."

We dashed over the ridge, and then along the hanging road, passed over the city on, as it were, a thread of rail. Clusters of towers and thousands of glittering metal roofs, mostly dome-shaped, and curious gardens full of trees of every form, were beneath our feet. Some of the gardens were on the roofs or on the fronts of houses, full of flowers, while between not a few of the towers were massive chains from which hung, here and there, baskets of creeping plants of every hue, which sent their perfume up to us. It was a beautiful scene of many colours and forms, where art used nature for her purposes; and nature, in that world, is as lovely as it is on earth, or even almost as with us, though so very different. The colours were richer and more glowing, and less delicate. But still they were splendid—deep crimsons, rich browns, dark purples, massive-looking greens. The air seemed full of hanging gardens of flowers and plants, beneath which, as through a net, one saw the many-shaped roofs of houses, and towers and spires of public buildings of every kind.

"It is something like a city of earth," I said to my companion, "but far more splendid. Paris, men think their finest city, but Paris is nothing to this."

We stopped at one of the towers, and then descended from our car. We went down the stairs into the city. The street was wide, but shaded from the sunlight by long avenues of red-leaved trees—or rather plants, for they were not trees like earth's trees, though vegetable products; their huge leaves spread over the road, and the sunlight glowed through them in blood-red tints. It was a scene such as would almost madden some human beings to dwell in that intense lurid glow, and yet it was glorious in its gorgeousness.

K

In the roadway, made partly of shining metal, partly of rocks laid out in mosaics of varied designs, and polished, there were many Martians going to and fro, some in cars, some on foot. Their cars were electric, for they use the master-force of nature very extensively, and employ it to cause the lesser and inferior forces, as heat, motion, magnetism, at will. The electric cars darted hither and thither on the metallic rails, with their violet sparks flashing from their electro-condensers, varying the scene of glowing splendour with their rapid motions. All around was glow, and motion, and sound; almost as great a contrast to the soft, sweet calm of our cities, as to the busy, but sad and gloomy tone of yours. And yet there was a something glorious about it; and I can easily fancy how those accustomed to such a world, and fitted for it, might immensely enjoy existence in such a cheering scene.

We entered through a massive arched doorway into a fine vestibule lighted by coloured windows. Thence we passed into a room where there reclined on a carpet a huge and majestic Martian of apparently venerable age, wrapt in a vast cloak. I noticed that these Martians showed their lion nature in reclining on the ground—crouching, as it were. Man

sits, for man is linked to the scansorial mammals, or the apes; but the Martians, in rest, lie
down, or crouch as lions on the floor. I was
presented to my strange host, who was told in
a few words my secret. He expressed surprise
at a being from our bright world having
crossed the vast chasm of space. When I
showed him really who I was, and cast off my
disguise, he asked me many questions, pre-
facing that I need only answer him on points
which were lawful to be spoken of. He
enquired much about the earth also, and entertained me some hours in conversation. Then
he gave me his blessing and wished me all
success, but bade me most earnestly not to
reveal myself, nor to let my secret be detected.

Evening was drawing in, and we went forth
again into the busy city streets. The electric
lights were shining on every side, and blazing
on the rich red foliage and the domes of the
houses. At length we came to the water-side.
On the green waves there were floating many
thousands of large vessels, of graceful shape.
My conductor led me to a little ship close by
the shore. We alone embarked on it. In a
few minutes an electric signal blazed from the
prow and we plunged forth on the Delarue
Ocean. Soon the lights of the ocean city grew

fainter in the distance and only the sea was around us, heaving with waves much like earth's ocean. Overhead there were the same stars as you know, but both the moons were shining together that night on the waters. We two were alone on the deep in our little electric ship.

We were not long out of sight of land. Lights, as of cities and towns, were on either side of us. We were passing up what you call Dawes Sea, between the two great Galileo and Huyghens' continents. The scene was such as I can scarcely describe. There is nothing on earth like it. Around us were the green waves, varied by forests of algæ of many colours, which tinted the waters into the semblance of a vast and glorious garden, while beyond, on either side of the long and narrow inlet were the ruddy shores of the two continents, with their crimson forests covering hill and dale, varied here and there by distant ranges of snow-capped mountains, soon lightened by the sun.

At length we came to an island rising out of the waters, with many vessels lying around it. It seemed quite built over. Thousands of towers and spires and domes of all glittering metals rose from the ruddy gardens—strange and majestic edifices with richly ornamented façades, as different to anything in our world as to the scenes of earth.

"That is the sacred city," said my guide, "the great centre of our religion, where the Holy One once dwelt when with us, and which we honour for His name. As you also are a servant of the One Eternal God, as you are a brother in the same Eternal Church that He has formed, I have brought you here to adore Him in our holy place, to pray in your own way, and in the way of your bright world, for God's blessing."

"It is well," I said. "I have prayed at Jerusalem, on earth; I now shall pray at the holy city of another world."

To prevent detection, we did not land till night had set in, and then we went from our little ship through strange scenes and processional avenues of mystic import to the great temple in the centre of the city. It was a magnificent edifice, but quite impossible for me to describe; huge in massive grandeur, richly ornate with singular designs of colossal size. It was partly of rock, partly of metal, and most of its ornaments were imitations of natural objects, for the Martians hold that the highest conception of beauty is in the works

of God, and the best they can do is to imitate
them.

It was a wonderful scene that opened to my
eyes as I passed that portal.   I had known for
ages the soft and peaceful worship of God in
our blissful world.   I had joined in the adoration of all the temples of our great cities.   I
had mingled my voice in the hymns of all the
nations of our world.   The grand ideal of our
adoration is peace and beauty and joy and
repose—the soul lost in an ecstasy of peace
and thankfulness.   I had also, as you know,
joined with men in their worship—imperfect,
like all things on earth are imperfect by man's
sin—and yet, in spite of all defects, having the
shadow of higher things.   I have adored in most
of your greatest fanes.   I have been at S.
Peter's when the silver trumpets have sounded
and the grandest music on earth has welcomed
the presence of the Pontiff.   I have seen
Cologne and Rheims.   I have mingled with the
adoring hosts in S. Isaac's at S. Petersburg and
the Cathedral of Kazan.   I have seen the
worship of the Armenian church of the Copts
and Abyssinians.   I have joined also with the
simpler worship of your English Church, more
like ours than the others on earth in being so
congregational, but unlike ours in being so

imperfect. I have been at S. Paul's and Canterbury, and York, and Ely, and your best churches. I have seen the worship of nearly all the Protestant sects—still more imperfect in beauty, still more didactic, but further still from ours in want of reverence and love, and beauty. I have even seen the most defective and darkened of the heathen rites—some of mingled causes, evidently of the earth most earthy; the temples of India, the mosques of Stamboul and Mecca.

But all these were unlike this new spectacle of the adoration of the creature to the Creator. It was as splendid as ours, but its splendour was gorgeousness, not repose; its spirit was passion, not peace; its aim was enthusiasm, not simple reverent love. Let me try to describe it, though I feel how defective earthly words are in describing any except earthly thoughts.

The Temple was vast and magnificent. A hundred thousand of the Martians were there in state robes of worship (for they specially vest for religious worship), the males on one side, the females on the other—two vast armies. The immense domes, to which your S. Paul's, and S. Peter's at Rome, were mere mole-hills, rose in exalted elevations over the heads of the hosts. All the walls, the pillars, the domes were encrusted with crystals of many colours, but all dimly visible in a dull light, which seemed to leave everything obscure.

The service began with a procession in gorgeous robes, and as they approached the central dome, the whole building shone in a blaze of electric lights; then from a hundred thousand voices burst the loud roar of song (too crushing to be melodious), and the blare of many trumpets made it seem as if the vast edifice could crush us. Then down on the ground the vast host fell adoring, and all died away, and there was silence. Then came soft, sweet melodies, and the light grew softened by degrees till we were again almost in darkness. Then again the host were silent, and one voice —a mighty voice, as speaking to us in silence and in darkness, was heard. I think I caught his words :—

"Adore Him, O creatures! Adore Him by Whom is all, in Whom is all, Whose ye are! Adore Him for His love! Soften and still the evil voice of passion in your souls, that all may be hushed before His presence!"

We did not stay long at the Holy City. My conductor seemed to doubt whether he ought to declare to me the mysteries of their religion, and I feared to enquire, for it is our belief that each of the worlds has its special dispensation designed by the great Creator of all, and that to enquire into the dispensation of God's will in other worlds would be mere curiosity, and harmful if not sinful. The same thought seemed to be in my conductor's mind. So I neither asked nor did he explain the strange mysterious sights we saw, and we merely passed through the city and saw its myriad worshippers crowding its vast streets, and the huge temples with their sacred symbols, some of which I could understand and some I could not. It was very grand and glorious altogether, though as different from the religion of our world as from yours. And yet truth is one as God is one, only the truth is reflected from different standpoints by divers minds. If, as you see, there is such a diversity of religions upon earth, you need not wonder at the variety of the reflections of truth in finite minds in other worlds. And yet amid the higher developments of being, the higher forms of mind, I have found more unity in the conception of things relating to God, *i.e.*, between ourselves and the Martians and the wisest and best of Christians, than I have found among men on the same earth; some of whom by stupidity misconceive the things relating to religion, and others by their sinfulness are obscured in their perception of it. So as in the material fabric of the worlds of our solar system there is an essential unity amid an infinite diversity, so in the conception of religion, there is an essential unity among the noble and good of all the worlds, though their modes of expression of their ideal may differ.

CHAPTER VI.

THE VOYAGE OF CIRCUMNAVIGATION.

WE sailed on over the Airy Sea till we saw the varied white and red outline of Laplace Land; white, because of the snows of the Arctic continent, but rendered most beautiful by the red vegetation, when the cold had not killed vegetable life. We crossed the Arctic circle in the Faye Sea, and then, bordered with glittering icebergs, shining in the sunlight rising from the green waters, the long ranges of snowy mountains of the Arctic continent appeared in all their grandeur. The scenery was very splendid, but, at the same time, not quite unearthly, for you have something like it even in Europe, in the northern shores of Norway, which so many now visit to watch the midnight sun. The red of Mars, however, is missing upon earth—the rich combinations of white and crimson—two of the most beautiful of colour combinations. The white slopes of the Arctic continent blushed like the cheek of a fair girl, brightened by a momentary excitement, while the green ocean and fantastic glittering icebergs formed a magnificent fringe to the blushing slopes of red and white.

We coasted for some days along the Arctic continent in these splendid scenes, passing sometimes vast submarine forests of algæ, which tinted the green waters, and made its colour change to such a degree that even your telescopes can notice these tinted spots upon the green ocean of Mars. The ocean was not lifeless. Amidst the icebergs sported huge monsters of the deep, and now and then electric ships of the Martians dashed past us.

At length (having sailed through what men call, from their astronomer's name, the Beer Sea) we crossed over from the icy Arctic continent, and its superb natural scenery, to what you call the Herschel continent. Here we sailed up the narrow channel between it and the Copernicus continent back to the warm and ruddy regions of the tropics. Sometimes the shores of both continents were in sight, with towers and cities rising out of the rich crimson forests. The hum of industry could be heard. The channel was filled with the electric ships. My companion told me the names

of the many cities we were passing till, crossing
the equator, we pushed on out of sight of land
to the great Newton Ocean. We crossed the
" tropic of the Lion " (for that is the southern
tropic of Mars, as yours is the tropic of
Capricorn), then came to the great island of
the Southern Ocean, which you call Secchi's
Land. The winter was coming on. Thousands
of vessels filled with their freights were sailing
down the Zollner Sea to bear the Martians of
Secchi's Land to more favoured lands. The
snow was already appearing. However, we
pushed on rapidly to near the antarctic circle,
where the sea was already nearly a mass of ice-
floes, into Philipp's Sea, just sighting the
antarctic isle (now clad in snow) of Rossland.
Then pushing down the Terby Sea, we once
more came in sight of Webb Land.

*   *   *   *

" Tell me," I said, " how you arrange your
exchanges of material things. On earth there
is a use of bits of gold and silver, which are
stamped to represent a certain amount of
things which are wanted, as food or clothes,
and people who have many of these bits of
gold are called rich ; but in our world of
Venus there is by a beneficent providence such
an abundance of everything that there is little

need of exchange, and all our gold and silver are used for ornament. How do you regulate the supply of things that are wanted ?"

"There was a time, when we were in our imperfect state, when war existed, and selfishness and all its evils, that we had a system of exchange and barter, and bought and sold, as it seems men do now. Each laboured for himself and his family, and for them alone. The strong prospered, and the weak suffered. But now we arrange that nothing shall belong to the individual, but all to the community. All that is wanted is supplied from the common stores."

"How do you provide against indolence ? On earth some theorists have held this view ; but it never has been found to answer—human selfishness is too great—each man would grasp all that he could from the common stores intended for all, and some would idle when others would have to work."

"We have stamped out selfishness in our world, or nearly so. The first point in the education of our little ones is to teach them to be truthful and unselfish. If, when they grow up, they are found to have failed to learn the lesson, we first punish them as liars or selfish, and if they are incorrigible, send them through the Tower of Doom out of our world. We pray for them, but we slay them. There is no room in our world either for liars or selfish people."

"It would be well if they could get rid of them on earth also. Men suffer crime to fester in their midst, and to pollute society. But tell me how do you govern your state?"

"By the rule of the wisest. Those who excel in wisdom and virtue are promoted to power; but they are never suffered to use their power for their own advantage, but for that of the community. We do not choose by popular election, but by competitive examination. The wisest of our mathematicians, and those who excel in calculation, are given the care of the treasures; those physicians who are proved to excel above others in physiology are given the care of sanitation; the most able architects the care of public buildings; the greatest botanists the care of the forests. The chief object of the state is to secure the greatest possible happiness to the greatest possible number, and to do this we require the highest available scientific knowledge in each department."

"I think you are wise. One of the greatest thinkers on earth—Plato—thought it would be best if philosophers were kings, or kings philosophers. Men now derive much of their trials and sorrows from giving power to political empirics, who know how to talk or to intrigue, or to toady, or to cringe and flatter, and then by their stupidity misapply the power entrusted to them, or else use it for their own selfish ends. You are wise in giving power to these who know the most. But is power hereditary with you, as in a majority of the lands of earth?"

"As long as the son proves himself worthy of a wise sire, I do not see why he should not possess his father's privileges; but we find sons and fathers often dissimilar, so we never put a son into his father's position until he has proved himself worthy of it."

"Then you do not recognise the family as the basis of society, as much as men do. I found among more cultured races, and especially in that continent so like your world, which men call America, a tendency against this family basis. But here is a danger from engendering selfishness by making individuals live for themselves and struggle for themselves. The strongest prosper, the weak are crushed."

"In our world duties are balanced. Each

individual has his duty defined to himself, to his family, to his village or civic community, to his nation, to the whole world. The community is the most important basis. The family is too small, the nation too large; but the sphere of duty is really balanced to all relations. In our earliest state each lived for himself. Then wars arose, and mutual assistance was required. Since we have had universal peace, we have tried to insist on each realising his duty to all society, and to the whole world."

"You spoke of common stores. How do you fill them?" I asked. "It seems to me there is a great deal more idle time and amusement in this world than on earth."

"Most of our work is done, as you see, by our control of natural forces. We convert the storm and the ocean wave into electricity, and by this we have a vast—almost an immeasurable —command of power. Thus, we can do our work, control and turn nature to our will, with little effort. So the more our control of the forces of nature has increased, the more leisure we have found for recreation, for development of the inner life, for study, for mental improvement, for relaxation. There was a time when our ancestors had to labour very hard, and life

L

was one round of endless toil. Then the rich
and the strong made the poor and weak labour
for them ; but since we have reached our present
state, we have been able to adjust labour wisely,
to give all their fair share of work and fair
share of healthy recreation, and to get our
efforts aided by the forces of nature subdued to
our will through the master force of electricity."

" You have done wisely," I said. " Perhaps
in time man may do the same, when he has
advanced further in knowledge."

" How do you divide the day in your com-
munes ?" I asked.

" One-third is given to work, if required
(which it rarely is), one-third to amusement
and refreshment, one-third to sleep. That is
on our working-days. On all feast-days there
is no work, but only recreation and devotion to
God's service. On working-days an hour out
of the working time is ever given to prayer and
praise."

" What do you understand by recreation ?"

" It is left to the individual taste. The
Government provides amusement. We have
no need now to fritter our means in armaments.
In every village, in every town there are bodies
of trained musicians, who nightly perform music

for their neighbours' amusement, for music we regard as an important element of happiness. Then every village has its theatre and its body of actors, where scenes are represented nightly for the recreation of the people. Then we have games of many kinds, mostly to develop the energy of the young. Lectures or speeches on subjects bearing on science are delivered by competent teachers. Then we have books and libraries for the enlightenment of all. Everything, of course, is provided by our rulers, one of whose chief duties is to provide healthy amusement and recreation for all. Then again, in most of our villages we take our meals together in a common hall. All work for the common good, and all are fed from the common stores. But to do this we must have perfect unselfishness."

"How do you manage with regard to the relation of the sexes? On earth this constant throwing young people together would be fraught with danger."

"Where the females are not taught modesty it would be so; but modesty and self-restraint are, after unselfishness, the first lessons we inculcate. But there is a great advantage in letting the young people of both sexes mix together, and know each other well before they marry. So we soften the character of the males by friendly and supervised conversation with the females."

"How do you manage about marriages? There is the chief difficulty in the societies of earth, and men have divers ways of dealing with it in divers nations."

"We expect those who wish to be married to know each other many years before the marriage is completed, and to obtain the consent of the elders."

*   *   *   *

We had many such conversations, which I cannot now describe to you, but the more he told me, the more I thought that in many things men might learn from the Martians—a class of beings not unlike men in many things, and living in a world very like your earth, but further advanced.

When passing Webb's Land, I asked if I might see one of the common feasts and recreations of the Martians. After some delay and consideration, my friend assented, on condition of my being very careful about preserving my secret, and not of exposing myself to detection. He promised to show me the Hall of Feasting and the Hall of Recreation of his own commune, when we got back to Tycho land, which we did next morning.

CHAPTER VII.

THE FEAST.

HE led me through a large garden, over-shadowed with ruddy foliage, amidst which could be seen flowers of every colour. It was a most gorgeous scene, but the colours were glaring and almost feverish—less pleasing to me far than the soft tints of our lovely world, and even than the grateful green verdure of the earth. Here all was glowing, and the very sunlight burst through leaves blood-tinted on the red ground. It was magnificent and gorgeous, but it had at last grown wearisome. Amid all this were the green cascades and fountains of the Martian waters, making a striking contrast to the red.

At length, about a mile off, we came to a large palace with lofty façade, flanked with metal towers. We entered its portals. There was a huge hall, as huge as any in Europe, with galleries around. Here were a number of Martians crouching on cushions on the ground.

My guide led me to a place, and here we sat down ready for a meal.

The loud blare of a trumpet sounded, and then a report as of a cannon. Then all stood as in an attitude of adoration, and there swelled a strange and mighty hymn of praise to God, the giver of all good. Then all reposed again, and the meals were laid before each—messes of food such as you have not on the earth, and as I cannot well describe. The very elements were somewhat different from those which men require in food. One thing was peculiar. With the meals was served out in cups a ruddy fluid of fragrant odour but metallic taste. I asked my guide what it was.

"It is a blood mixture, made by science to represent the elements of our blood. In our early and defective state, when war existed in our world, we used to kill animals, and even drink their blood. We were to a great extent carnivora. Now this is changed. Science provides us the same elements as flesh, and we can live on mere fruits with the aid of this metallic compound, which is more grateful, and I think more suitable, than the flesh or the blood of dead animals. It does just as well."

After the feast, we went forth into the next hall, and I saw many strange sights not easy to describe. The Martians seemed a race full of energy and of high development. Many games of skill were going on, and as the young Martians cast off their garments, I saw that they were really not so entirely like men as they seemed when clothed. Their limbs were more muscular, and they had more hair about them than human beings. When clad as I said, they were extremely like men. Their heads were quite human in intelligence, but their lower limbs showed as much resemblance to the carnivora as the human limbs do to the quadrumana.

I passed from here into another hall—very splendid and ornate—where music was going on, and then into another, where a drama was being performed. Another hall was beyond, where science was expounded, and beyond this we came to a library with books. Everything showed that the Martians, though they had to work (as men have), still strove to make life pleasant.

*　　　*　　　*　　　*

It is impossible for me to describe all the strange sights I beheld on Mars, while I traversed again, with my Martian friend, the oceans of this strange world. Earthly words are only fit for earthly things, and so are imperfect and, therefore, deceptive, when applied to the things of another world. There were, however, many matters on which you might learn from the people of your sister orb. The main point I learnt there was, that all our three worlds are in many points akin, but that earth is the least happy of the three. With us little evil exists; on Mars, though there may once have been quite as much as on earth, and the Martians quite as wicked as men, yet nearly all great evils have been put down and stamped out by the courage and good sense of the Martian rulers. If we are better than men, the Martians are braver, and so have crushed evil which you have left to fester horribly, and render earth one of the most miserable of the many worlds that roll around the King of Day —our mighty sun.

I saw, on my journey, many wonderful things —great cities; long, straight ranges of hills, and equally straight lines of inlets and sounds of green sea; forests and fields of many forms and of varied vegetations; hundreds of fine rivers, of green waters, and canals without number. The land of Mars is nearly as exten- sive as that of earth (the seas being much less), and so there is as much to see of interest on Mars as on your world; indeed, there is more

—larger populations, more developed civilisation, a society more advanced in intelligence, progress, and good government than any you have ever yet known on earth.

Thanks to my friend, I was enabled to see a good deal, and yet to keep my secret unsuspected; but, except on the occasion I mentioned, in his own village and at his request, never went to any place of public resort, nor did I venture to converse with the Martians, except when obliged to do so. I thus had more restraint put on me than in your world, where I managed to disguise myself perfectly, and mix freely with mankind. I appeared only as a child under the tutelage of my guide, and such a disguise was essential to me.

At length, having seen much of this strange and beautiful world, we returned to Tycho Island, and I parted, with many prayers and blessings for his welfare, from my kind Martian friend. I again joined my companions, Ezariel and Arauniel, whom I found near where I had left them in the rendezvous awaiting me. They had seen most of the natural beauties of the planet, having flown from mountain to mountain, mostly by night and at great heights, resting in remote and inaccessible places, lest they should be discovered. Perhaps they had

had more bird's-eye views than I had had. They had visited both the North and South Pole, even in the regions of perpetual ice. Once they had noticed me sailing in our little vessel over the Terby Sea. Their far-seeing instrument had enabled them to detect me at a great distance, but they had purposely made no sign by which I might recognise them. They had examined the peaks of the loftiest mountains of Mars, and had flown over most of the great cities both by night and by day. Once or twice they thought they had been noticed by the Martians, but on each occasion had soared out of sight directly. They had also collected many specimens of curious things.

We flew together to the mountain where we had left our ether-car, and then, once more developing the anti-gravitating power, darted forth into space.

PART IV.—THE GIANT WORLDS.

———

CHAPTER I.

DEIMOS, AND THE VOYAGE FROM MARS THROUGH SPACE.

HIGHER and higher did we rise from the Ice Mountain. At our feet the green expanse of the Delarue Ocean opened wider and wider, with the verdant billows rolling one after another in long lines, like the huge pampa-grass of your American plains, with now and then a white snow-cloud resting on expanse.

Higher and higher we rose, till the red cliffs of Schroeter's land were in sight, and the white and red plains of Tycho's Island now dappled by snow, with the Lockyer Sea in its centre, and then the wide ruddy plains of the Copernicus, Galileo, and Huyghens' continents. Still higher and higher, till, from a sea of green, the world we had left seemed, as it does to you, of red and white, the ruddy plains and forests glowing

like fires beneath the blazing sun. It looked
very rich and gorgeous in its varied colours—a
splendid and majestic spectacle; none the less
so, because every point we could see had now
for us some pleasing reminiscence of what we
had beheld when viewing it more nearly.
Higher still we went, till Mars seemed as a
huge globe beneath our feet.

Our first start was, as I said, for the moon
of Deimos, one of the two little satellites of
Mars. It is one of the smallest of the worlds
of the solar system, for few even of the planetoids are so minute. Its surface is smaller
than that of the Isle of Wight. London might
have almost covered one of its hemispheres,
and Paris would have taken up a great part of
it. It was a half-moon when we approached it,
and its aspect, part black as night, part shining
in the sunlight, was very striking. At first it
seemed as a huge balloon rolling through space;
but, as we drew nearer, the rocks and cliffs
showed it a tiny world, hardly deserving the
name of world, were it not for its regular orbit
and its position in space as definite a satellite
as, comparatively, huge Titan or your Moon.

The aspect of Deimos is very striking. Its
size is so small, that you feel that it is a globe
even when upon it; indeed, it appears little
more than a colossal meteor, an expanse of

rock and rugged cañons of piled cliffs and stones. We rested on one of its largest rocks, and thence surveyed the dreary little world around us, and the great ruddy planet, with its green seas and its snow-clad hills, and polar ice and glaciers. It was a lovely sight! Mars is so glorious in colour—one of the loveliest, the most varied, the most gorgeous of the many worlds that roll around the mighty sun. In other worlds one colour is prevailing: on the earth blue and green; in our lovely Venus white, and the paler, or more glowing tints; but in Mars all colours save blue—the very antithesis to the earth, where blue is dominant. Mars has the dominant hue of red, and the earth of blue.

Glorious he looked from that tiny moon, and from its rugged cliffs and rocks, and as we rolled on around him, like a moving panorama, he opened to us new splendour. Seas, continents, oceans, and mountain chains, ruddy plains and green lakes, all dappled by the white fleecy clouds, and, in some places, glittering with snows—all appeared before us as we moved with more than railway speed around this world. It was like a balloon view of earth, only on a far vaster scale. The motions of Phobus, the other satellite, varied the scene as he also dashed through space

around the gorgeous and many-coloured orb—
the sovereign world to both. It was a wonderful and splendid scene of glowing hues, and in
the evening, when the stars decked the sky,
the cities' lights made it appear hardly less
glorious than by day.

We lingered several days on that tiny moon,
rolling round the ruddy planet, thus watching
the oceans and continents opening to our
vision. There was a fascination in the scene,
so that we could hardly tear ourselves from it.
It was like rolling in a car through space—a car
so small and rapid that one felt and perceived its
motion, which one cannot do in larger satellites.

As we spent our time watching Mars, we
also compared notes. I told my companions
of my travels, and pointed to them the cities
and long lines of roads of Mars. They in their
turn showed me the natural treasures they had
collected—the plants, the rocks, the smaller
animals. They explained the variations of
nature they had observed, the operation of the
natural laws, the combinations of the elements.
They pointed out to me the lakes and rivers,
the mountains and morasses of Mars, and told
me of the measures they had taken and the
wonders they had seen in the many ruddy
lands that we saw rolling before us.

Then at length Ezariel, wearied at our long delay and our rapt dwelling upon Mars, said: "Let us behold more. Perchance, Mars is not to be compared with the mightier orbs beyond. Let us go on—forward into space to behold new splendours, new miracles of Divine love and power."

We assented to the justice of what he said, and tore ourselves unwillingly from the ruddy orb and its tiny satellite, and went onwards into space. We put our machine into action. The compensating force was set against gravitation. The little moon and the orb of Mars lost their attractive power, and we launched into infinity—far into the black ether, studded with its myriads of distant systems—the huge measureless ocean of the infinite. The satellite Deimos rushed away from us in his course around Mars, and we plunged in our little ether-car into infinity.

Our first work, as before, was to seek for one of the meteoric streams rolling away from the sun. We soon, flying through ether, came on one of these—a long crowd of rocks, poised in space, rolling on through ether around the sun in an ellipse. We attached our car to one of the larger of these, and then swept on with it.

The journey was long, and would have been somewhat tedious had we not had abundant occupation in arranging the wonders we had collected in the ruddy world we had left behind. The rock, or meteor, on which we rested offered but little to employ us. It was but a few scores of yards across, and was formed irregularly. It was a mass of iron and manganese, chromium, and sodium. Still it was easier than the ether-boat we had attached to it. Sometimes we landed on it, sometimes remained in the ether-car. We analyzed its rocks, and examined microscopically their texture, and found in them vestiges of infusorial life of many orders.

On, on we went; on towards the vast system of worlds to which we aimed. On day by day (speaking of the earth or Venusian days), up to a year, ever forward we flew, with the long flow of myriads of meteors around us dimly reflecting the sunlight, and Jupiter slowly growing larger and brighter, till we tfelt hat we might get within his influence.

Then Ezariel called us into the ether-boat, and he detached it from our friendly little rock, and we launched out again into space. But now purposely the anti-gravitating power was not used. We were within the influence of the planet and his vast mass. We rushed through space as fast as a cannon-ball fired from a rifle cannon—hundreds of miles a minute—on towards the great world before us.

CHAPTER II.

FIRST IMPRESSIONS.

WE went with terrific rapidity to that huge globe, which constantly grew huger, with his four moons—rather planets than moons—rolling round him.

The orb of Jupiter was evidently wrapt in clouds—long lines and belts, and broken spaces here and there, through the masses of mist, in which we hoped to see the planet himself.

At length we felt we were getting into his cloud-land. The force of gravitation had then to be compensated. "If we," said Arauniel, "strike land like this, we shall pierce into the depths like a bullet for many yards. Back with the pressure! Undo the gravitating power!" We did so. Still the momentum was terrific. Swift into the clouds we dashed. Long miles of floating vapour were passed through in a few moments. It seemed as a dream, a mere gauze veil. Then a momentary glance at a vast expanse of heaving, tempestuous ocean, overcast with overhanging piles of clouds, then a tremendous splash, and we were rushing into the waters of the ocean of the great planet.

To any man it would have been instant death, but we have, as you know, far mightier vitality than man's, and under the waters we can live for a long time. Still, the crash was inconvenient to us, and when the resistance of the waters had quieted our onward motion, Ezariel again put the force of impetus to the ether boat upward, and we rushed up again out of the ocean depths to the planet's surface, the boat glowing with heat caused by friction, and the waters hissing in a cloud around us. We rose, therefore, in a vast whirlpool, with great clouds of steam rising from the heated depths, until again we came to the surface.

It was a vast ocean in which we found ourselves. The waves rose to the height of real mountains, and sank again. We floated on this tempestuous sea, such as the earth in its worst hurricane has never seen, hoping sometimes, as we were swept upwards on a mountain-like crest, to catch a sight of land, but none could we see.

Having thus floated for some time, Arauniel proposed that we should rise into the air, and

by flying over the surface seek for land. We
flew up to a moderate height, under the clouds.
The wind was not so violent as the waves
would imply, and even they were going down
now. So we managed to fly in the air, floating
beneath the clouds over the tempestuous waves.
Our ether-car floated rapidly, like a balloon,
over the great heaving mountains of the mighty
waters,—like a mountainous region, but all in
motion,—peaks and cliffs of foam ever rising
and falling.

Long we floated, over many thousands of
miles, but nothing save liquid mountains, hundreds of feet high, and dark ocean valleys were
in sight. No land, nor trace of land, did we
see. At length Arauniel called out from the
top that he saw an island. It appeared really
to be one, but very small—just like a large
rock on the sea, a few hundred yards across.

We descended and landed on the island. It
was not firm. In a moment we felt its heaving
as it was shaken by the waves. It was evidently
of some light substance, floating upon the
waves. Still, putting our ether ship into a
cleft, we rested awhile, watching the strange
scene of the tempestuous waves and the vast
overhanging clouds, and every moment were
reminded of the primæval chaos, such as our

world and the earth were in in the remote ages, before the time when lands and continents were defined, and when all was yet unformed. "Surely," said Arauniel, "this huge planet has not yet attained its solid state, like Earth and Mars and our world."

After some hours of wondering at this scene, we were inclined to explore our floating islet. One of the first things we noticed was an enormous cavern of a hundred feet high in the rock. We entered it, and passed into a huge hall, the extent of which partly explained the floating power of the island, for it was practically as hollow as an ironclad, and if the walls were heavier than water, the hall made it lighter and gave it buoyancy. The hall was colossal in proportions—much larger than any cathedral I have seen on earth. On one side of it was a large terrace, and the surface was damp, though the waters in mass were well kept out of it. The roof was vaulted. Huge arches were raised of the massive rock, and the dripping waters had formed vast stalactites, These was a certain grandeur and beauty, however, in this rocky cavern, as we examined it by the electric light, which Ezariel took with him. At the end were two great openings, which might possibly lead to more huge caverns in the rock.

As we were admiring the cavern, suddenly a strange gigantic being entered the open door. He was of colossal height, rational and erect in aspect, yet strangely fish-like also. A vast monster of the deep, yet apparently something more than a mere brute. His body was covered with scales. His head was not altogether stupid, and he had a forehead and walked erect like a man. I can best describe him as like what one of the huge beings of the secondary formation of earth—of the oolite or lias—would have been if endowed with intelligence and reason ; yet he was more symmetrical in aspect, and therefore more beautiful, than they ever were. He evidently was of the type of life which in the earth is still seen in the huge monsters of the deep, and yet he looked in aspect semi-human—like to the fabled Titans of the old Greek poets—a monarch of the deep, colossal and majestic, yet for all that oceanic.

He entered the cavern dripping with water, and at once seated himself on the terrace. He rested back as if weary, and leaning on the rock sank off to sleep.

This gave us a chance of examining him. We mounted the terrace and contemplated his huge limbs at our pleasure. He was evidently formed to live in the water—rather to swim than to walk, and certainly not to fly. The pressure of gravitation of the huge planet made us feel that swimming was the most suitable mode of existence there. To walk was an effort, for one wanted a resisting medium, and this huge body was formed for the purpose of floating in the waters, or for plunging into its depths.

As we thus surveyed him with our electric lamp, which on his entry we had extinguished, another gigantic being entered the cave, and resting on another terrace also sank to sleep. The cavern darkened. We went to the opening. Night—the short night of Jupiter—was setting in. The sky was covered with stars, and three of the four moons were shining on the heaving waters. It was a wondrous scene —that ocean and its heaving waves, and the starry sky with those three moons shining in it.

On we went over the heaving ocean-surface, on for hundreds of miles. Now and then, however, floating islands did appear, heaving on the oceanic waves. Some of them appeared not to be natural, but artificial—the work of created intelligences; on some of these (as we were floating in the air) we could see the colossal Jovians resting on them. These islands were not like the ships of earth, merely for floating on the surface, but sometimes they sank suddenly into the deep and as suddenly appeared on the surface.

I noticed the difference to Ezariel. " Men float on the surface because they want air to breathe. If they could live under the surface, they would doubtless sink into the deep, and construct ships to do so, like these huge ships, which seem to us floating islands of the Jovians." *

We resolved also to explore the depths of the vast ocean.

---

* There are three classes of views about Jupiter. (1) That which is held by Mr. Proctor, that it is an un- formed world, and therefore as yet unfitted for life. (2) That of Swedenborg, that the inhabitants of the greatest of the planets are of superior nature. This can- not be refuted, as thereby they would be superior to the destructive agencies at work on the planet. (3) M. Flam- marion's view, that life is here " manifested under strange forms, in beings both vegetable and animal of astonishing vitality, in the midst of the convulsions and storms of a developing world" is the one I would favour. It is hard to believe this huge world a lifeless desert, though terrestrial life (such as we have on earth) could not exist there.

CHAPTER III.

THE OCEAN WORLD.

DOWN into the deep we sank. On-rushing through miles of water. As we passed onwards thousands of strange monsters of the deep met our sight, swimming about here and there, single and in shoals. Most of them appeared as irrational as the great fishes of earth. Some were reptilian in aspect, more like the ichthyosaurus or the cetiosaurus of the secondary formation of earth than any earthly fish. Some were apparently higher in type, like the whales or dolphins of the earth's oceans.* But a few appeared of rational nature, and were provided with singular implements of swimming, alone, or elsewhere floating in sub-marine ships of metal, curiously designed, and propelled through the waters with great velocity.

* "They are aqueous, gelatinous creatures, too sluggish almost to be deemed alive, floating in their ('ice-cold') waters (of Saturn and Jupiter), shrouded for ever by their humid skies."—"*Plurality of Worlds,*" 301.

At length we came to a strange scene of aquatic vitality such as I never dreamt of, and such as I can scarcely describe. It seemed like an island in the waters. It was manifestly not the solid bottom, like the bottom of the earth's ocean. Huge walls and towers appeared, vast and massive, as one might expect in the hugest world of all our solar system. Amidst them swam hundreds of vast forms, dashing hither and thither in the waters. It was a scene of bustle, and motion, and activity, yet all most strange.

"Nothing we have yet seen is like this," said Ezariel. "Neither in Mars nor in our own home."

"Nor yet the earth or her satellite," I said. "This is a world of waters. All other peoples we have seen live on the surface. These dwell evidently in the depths of their huge world. To them the waters are as the air to us."

"And might we not have expected this?" replied Ezariel. "Have we not known for ages, that this giant world was very light in its gravitating power, considering its size? It appears a liquid sphere, or system rather, as the mighty Sun is a vast orb of gases or metals fused into a gaseous state. In our world, as on Earth and Mars, all three states of matter exist fairly proportioned—the solid, the liquid and the gaseous; in the Earth's Moon you say you only found the solid; in the Sun there seems to be only the gaseous; why should we not here expect to find the liquid dominant—a world in which the fluid prevails as with us the solid? Now we can understand the sudden changes we have seen, even in a single night, upon this vast globe—his shifting belts, his spots forming and dissolving in a few hours—the most wondrous example (save the mighty Sun himself) of vast and rapid change in our system; now we can understand his lightness, his comparatively small gravitating power, perhaps even his brilliancy."

"There must be an advantage in this," said Arauniel, "to these huge beings, some of whom seem endowed with intelligence. They are not bound to the surface as men or the Martians are, or near the surface as we; they can traverse their world up and down—down into its inner depths for hundreds of miles."

"On earth," I replied, "they partially feel this advantage of the waters. It is true, man has never yet obtained that sovereignty over the sea that he has over the land. But still the sea is of use to man. It is the great highway of commerce. Upon the sea he carries much of his products. The dominion of the sea confers on the nation that holds it a supremacy and power that other nations have not. The sea is a great civiliser, for the ports of many of the wilder regions of the earth are far more civilised than the interior regions ; and the last strongholds of barbarism and savagery will probably be the inland parts of Africa. From the sea man gathers much of his food. One of the greater problems of his future on Earth, perhaps, is the utilisation of the ocean to his purpose. On Earth there are, as it were, two worlds of life—the terrestrial and marine ; and of these the marine is the larger, though the less important. Each world has its animal and vegetable kingdom, with their orders, families, general species, as distinct as though they belonged to different planets."

" Then it seems," said Ezariel, " that Earth must be a sort of mean between this world and the solid Moon. In Mars we have seen a world where land is quite dominant, though sea exists. May there not be a law in this? The larger worlds more fluid, the smallest solid, the medium ones mixed ?"

Our conversation had an abrupt termination. One of the huge Jovians at length perceived our ether-car, and, rapidly swimming to it, strove to grasp it. Seeing the danger of our capture, and not knowing how we might fare with these huge beings, for once we felt helpless and overcome. But we had provided for such a possible danger. In our car we had, as I said, vast command of electrical forces. Seeing the peril, I at once set the electricity in full force. As he grasped our car, the shock rolled him back into the waters.

Then we set the full motive-power at work. Up we dashed through the deep. For a moment it seemed as if the Jovians would pursue us, for several noticed our ether-car. But we rushed on, defying pursuit towards the surface. Rapidly we dashed upwards through the waste of dark waters, till at last the great billows of the surface could be felt heaving to and fro, and then we rushed up into the air through masses of hissing foam.

We rose from the surface into the mist-lands beneath the clouds.

"It is well," said Ezariel, "we have escaped those Jovian giants of the deep; but it is sad to think that we cannot hope to know them as we did the Martians. Their nature is too distinct from ours for us to understand them, or to make them understand us. And yet this huge world of waters, like everything in creation, appears wonderfully suited for its object."

"How different each world is from all the others," said Arauniel; "and yet each, doubt-less, in its way, most admirably adapted. Our fair world is very different from that gorgeous world of Mars; and, from your account, Earth, and the dead world of the Moon are very different from each; and now this giant world is utterly different from all the others."

"Not utterly," I said, "there is an under-lying unity beneath all this diversity."

CHAPTER IV.

THE LAND OF FIRE.

WHEN we came to the surface, we again resolved to rise into the air. We rose over the mighty heaving ocean of the giant planet.

"There is no chance," said Arauniel, "of conversing with these huge beings, as we did on the gorgeous planet we have left. Whatever may be their polity, their thoughts, their faith, their hopes, we cannot know. They seem of another order to us,—another class of beings. The inner and lesser planets, such as the Earth, or our own planet of love, and the one we have left, all have much alike, and so life in them is like; but here we have life of another type, and one with which we cannot well communicate."

"Not quite another type," I said. "On earth, as I told you, they have this type, but in a low and soulless state, in the fishes of the ocean. In the earlier ages of the earth it was more developed than now. Men now place these fish in aquaria, and watch their movements. The scene we have just beheld somewhat reminds me of the monsters of Earth's ocean,—of the type of life in their seas. Here it is still more gigantic,—still more marvellous; and it would seem that in these huge frames intelligences are enshrined it may be, for aught we know, of a nobler order. That crystal city was grand and wonderful; design and beauty was there, but of strange kind. It is not for us to judge these singular, vast beings, whom we cannot understand."

"It looks like the fish type exaggerated and developed," said Ezariel.

"But is there not some truth in the old beliefs of mankind on the Earth, which are now exploded—of Titans, and Mermaids, and ocean-beings endowed with life and intelligence? On Earth there are none such, and never were; but it may be that man, by inspiration, or by instinct, or by contact with spirits superior to himself, has gained the thought of such a type of life as this endowed with intelligence. On earth once it was the hugest type of life, and still it is so, for the animals of the sea are greater than on the land."

"What is this light to which we are

coming ?" said Ezariel. "I see a vast fire raging over the sea."

Then we looked from our windows and saw, far over the heaving waves, a long line of blazing fire, as of huge masses burning.

" Perhaps this world," said Arauniel, " is still unformed. As you saw in the Moon a dead world, worn out, exhausted, where life is destroyed and finished with,—here may be an imperfect world, a huge mass yet developing, which has not thoroughly cooled."

"Perhaps so," I replied, "as upon the Earth it would seem, when the cooling process had gone on for many ages, the sea was first inhabited by living beings, before the land was properly formed."

" One thing has struck me," he said, " ever since I came here,—the much greater heat of this world than we expected. Men, as you say, supposed that this giant planet would be too cold for an abode of life because it is so far from the Sun, and yet now the air is far hotter than it is even in our own sunny world, and even the tropics of Earth are never so hot as this. But the heat here is plainly internal, not solar. It is from Jupiter himself, and not from the Sun."

" There is one origin of the heat plainly,"

N

said Ezariel, pointing to the blazing, copperous-looking fires.

"The heat is like the blast of a furnace," I said. "It reminds me of Hecla on Earth in a state of eruption; but no Earth-volcano for many thousands of years has ever blazed like this. The air would even now be insupportably hot to any terrestrial animal. Men would call this the heat of boiling water, and still we are miles off. Had we not better turn away from this eruption? The instruments will soon be affected by the heat, and some of our collections destroyed."

Ezariel consented, and we upraised the ether-car a mile or two, the better to contemplate the terrific conflagration. There were rising out of the waters, surrounded by huge piles of scoriæ and ashes, some hundreds of miles of blazing flames and incandescent matter. Out from the deep rushed vast columns of smoke and steam and ashes, whilst glowing rivers of lava flowed towards the hissing seas, which, in a cloud of mist and steam, from time to time enveloped the volcanoes. Stromboli, Vesuvius, Etna, Hecla, indeed all the volcanoes of either hemisphere on Earth together, in full eruption, would not produce such an effect as this.

PART V.—SATURN.

CHAPTER I.

TITAN.

Look then abroad through nature to the range of planets, suns, and adamantine spheres, wheeling unshaken through the void immense.

WE ascended from the wondrous scene of the fire-land and vast, hissing mists, and the huge waving sea of the giant planet. We pierced the regions of clouds around him, and at length we came to the vast, black expanse of ether, studded by a million stars. Again we launched into the infinite.

Thus once more we plunged into space— infinite space,—dark, airless ether, with the myriads of glittering stars far off on every side. Again we got upon a meteor ring, and swept on through space toward the mighty system of the Ringed World. The journey was long—

days and weeks and months, by your earth-measurement of time, passed on this weary voyage. Still Saturn seemed little more than a great star in space, with its mighty rings and its eight moons slowly growing more and more distinct. On, still on, we swept, away from the great orb of day, the Sun, which slowly grew less and less glorious. As we travelled onwards, we compared our experiences of the worlds we had seen, and examined the relics of them we had collected. The conclusion we came to was that which I had anticipated : the solar system is one, yet it is unity in diversity. The elements of matter are the same—the metals, the rocks, the main forms are one, as springing from the same great nebula of primæval chaos. But the combinations differ. Even in the Giant World we had left there was nothing really and essentially new to us, except in form and combination. The origin was the same, the main points of being identical, but an infinite variety in combination.

So also with life. We had seen no really new forms of life. Even on your Earth they are to be traced, though often imperfect and low in development. As the worlds were the same, or very nearly the same, in metallic elements, in spherical shape, in motion, in atmospheres, in gravitation, in electricity—so also in the vitality on their surfaces.

TITAN AND MIMAS.

At length we came within the influence of the great Ringed World, and felt ourselves dashing towards it by the mighty power of gravitation. Like three huge rainbows in the starry sky appeared the mighty rings—vast tracks of nebulous matter cast off by the planet in its rapid whirl. "Such rings as these," Arauniel said, "were probably once around all the exterior planets. Around Jupiter, where the four moons sometimes still remind us of them; around little Mars, even when Deimos and Phobos were in formation; around the Earth, when the Moon was being cast off into space in palæozoic times. All once were ringed worlds, but they have passed that stage of being. Yet here we have a very ancient world still by its own inherent power retaining the ring formation,—a last relic of a primæval stage of world-existence."

As we rushed forward, we felt the force of attraction drawing us from our onward course.

We were deflecting towards one of the minor worlds that rolled around that great ringed system. It was the chief of them—the satellite you call Titan, the greatest of the satellites of our solar system, greater than the world Mercury himself. On, on we flew, on to this lesser world, worthy of being a follower of the great Sun, but now a satellite of Saturn.

" Let us rest on one of the mountains," said Arauniel, "and watch this wonderful system— a miniature of our own great solar system, with yon huge world as a minor sun, around which these eight worlds roll, and the three rings around his surface marking that which once circled on a smaller scale the Earth and Mars."

We flew on towards this moon, not so very much less than the earth itself. Continents and oceans were stretching far and wide beneath its clouds.

It was a strange world—primitive in formation, imperfect in development. I cannot well describe the wonders we there saw. The marvels of its heavens were great, and the wonders of its surface greater still. It was, as it were, a world of double suns—the one, the glorious Sun, now shining, with rays feebler far than those which you know in the arctic regions of the earth; the other the great ringed sun of Saturn, far larger and more majestic, with his triple walls of light girding him like a huge

citadel enclosed in triple lines of fortifications.
And there also were to be seen the seven sister-
satellites, that followed like seven great planets,
while beyond there were the planets we were
wont to see in the heavens and our own world
and earth now fading in the distance. Yet all
were indistinct compared with the great system
of Saturn around us.

We quitted this giant satellite before Titan
had made a quarter revolution around his
primary—the great belted and ringed world,—
and plunged into the system itself, passing by
four of the moons, — Rhea, Dione, Tethys,
and Enceladus,—until we came to the little
world of Mimas, where we rested again.

I cannot describe the strange things of that
world of Mimas. Earthly words depict only
earthly things, or at best only things of nature
akin to those of earth. But here there were
other forms of development, other conditions
of life, and other resultants than such as you
find on earth. And yet, just as the minerals of
that world were much the same as we have and
as you have, though in quite strange combinations, so the elements of life were somewhat
the same, though in the dull, imperfect light,
less developed in their higher forms. One
thing was singular, however, which I had not

noticed yet,—the higher living creatures of that
world neither walked as the animals of the
dominant type of life on Earth or Mars, nor
flew as we do in the dense atmosphere of our
glorious mountain world, nor were chained to
the depths as the huge beings of the giant
planet, but sprang. I asked Arauniel why
should this be. "It is the effect of gravitation. Do not you feel how light you are?
You see on this world there are two forces
at work—the moderate gravitation of Mimas
and the less but still felt power of Saturn.
One gravitation partly neutralises the other.
So by slight exertion these beings leap,—they
neither need to walk nor fly; a slight effort
overcomes their gravitation. Here, practically, all things belong to two worlds, the little
satellite on which they dwell and the mighty
planet, like a giant globe (many times the
size of the sun in our skies), above them."

The evenings in that little world were
wonderfully glorious. There, ever through
the sky, were rolling the huge orb and his
three rings, and the seven sister-moons ever
varying in their phases.

There was nothing here, it seemed, to detain
us, save wonder; there was nothing beautiful
nor sublime in this world, only things quaint

and strange. However, the heavens above and the changes there were wonderful. So we rested on a mountain far removed from the lower manifestations of life which filled the plains,—those wierd beings that seemed with little effort to rise from the surface and go where they would.

* * * *

I can hardly describe our final journey into the realm of Saturn—the voyage from Mimas to the huge central orb itself. Nothing had we beheld more magnificent or awe-inspiring than those gigantic rings. There was a solemn sense at the approach to the outer ring. We drew near to it purposely, but as we approached nearer its solid appearance dissolved. Rents here and there appeared in its surface, and what looked solid at a distance was manifestly composed of millions of fragments of matter, meteors in millions were sweeping onwards in many streams. If there be anything on earth to which I might liken it, it would be the Lake of a Thousand Islands, only the islands were not rocks rising out of the waters, but shining meteors in space, and the medium in which they floated was ether, not water. As swarms of bees, the millions of meteors rolled on in space around the huge belted orb of Saturn.

CHAPTER II.

SATURN.

Here Nature first begins
Her farthest verge and chaos to retire,
As from her outmost works a broken foe
With tumult less and with less hostile din.
                    MILTON'S *Paradise Lost.*

O N, on we went through space towards that
vast belted globe, the great rings rising
overhead like a huge aurora, and the moons
in a vast corona around. It grew huger and
huger, till its glistening clouds formed a vast
expanse before us, and the belts of Saturn grew
into huge openings. Into one of these we
dashed. The scene of that outer region of mist
was not unlike that of the great planet we had
left—Jupiter. It seemed as if we were ever
going on and on for hundreds of miles, with the
huge seas of mist rising around us. At length
we came to a resistance, as of some solid expanse of matter, through which we dashed, and
then felt our further progress stopped in a great

morass, in which our vessel sank. We had some difficulty in extricating it, by using all the force we had in the stored electric force of the machine. When we reached the surface again, it was indeed a strange scene that met our eyes. A huge forest, as it seemed, of gigantic plants was there in rank luxuriance. They looked akin to the lower orders of Earth's vegetation—something like gigantic lichens—in nature, or rather in position in creation, not remote from the forms of vegetation that formed your coal-shales. All were of low type, but of colossal size, such as would suit a world in process of formation,—such as existed on your world in the carboniferous age,—such as our world and, possibly, Mars once knew, when in their earlier stages of development.

" Strange it is," I said, " here in these giant planets we have worlds that seem in the state of formation which we know our world and Earth once passed through; and yet in some of the satellites (for instance, in the Earth's Moon), we find finished, worn-out, dead worlds. How can this be if, as it seems, this world of Saturn is a more ancient world than ours, thrown off long ago by the sun ?"

" Perhaps it is simply," said Arauniel, " because this world and Jupiter are so huge that they have more independent existence,—more difficulty in developing, so as to suit the higher types of life. Here we evidently have a very early type of world. Not only has it eight satellites, but you see it even retains the ring which Earth and Jupiter once had, but which ages ago they lost. All here is antique and archaic, as, indeed, men foresaw in their theories of astrology. Here one may study the *juventus mundi*—an antique, primitive, undeveloped, half-chaotic world."

He had scarcely finished, when beneath the huge shadow of the giant fungi appeared a strange and terrible creature—inchoate like all around, huge in size and ill-formed in aspect,—something of the insect type, but colossal. It moved towards us. For once we felt horror. I had, alas! felt it on earth before, in scenes of woe and crime. But here we felt there was a creature of huge strength, yet of nature not akin to ours. Whether he had intelligence I cannot say. He moved among the gigantic fungi to our ether-car, and then moved it with his .huge ciliated limbs. His aspect was horrible. After staying and looking at it with seeming curiosity—though it may be no more than a mere animal might feel at a thing strange and unknown,—he let it go, and then passed on into the huge forest of colossal fungi and lichens.

This was not the only denizen of the forest. Strange forms still appeared, such as men never think of save in nightmares: some gigantic, some of more moderate dimensions, but none apparently of any nobleness of aspect; nothing like what we had seen in other worlds, and all seemed of inferior types, or rather developments in great size of the inferior types of life. We remained in our car, watching these strange beings pass and re-pass.

"This seems," I said, "like some of the dreams of Dante's 'Inferno.' These horrid, inchoate forms are what men dreamt of in the Middle Ages as the eternal companions of the spirits of the wicked. Is this a region given up to sin,—a world more fallen than Earth even, —a realm in rebellion against God?"

"Not necessarily so," said Ezariel; "it may be only a region undeveloped as yet, where Nature is imperfect,—where as yet she cannot produce her masterpieces. It may be that the higher forms of being may even thus be developed in these strange types."

"It would seem," I said, "as if there was some little ground in the notion of the old astrologers of Earth, that this vast planet is inimical in its influence. Saturnine is used even now among men as a term for dark, harsh, evil influences. It may have been that it was because this planet, removed from the Sun's rays, is less brilliant than the others, or it may have been that Man, by some higher instinct or revelation, knew that it was of a form of creation distinct from Earth."

"In one sense it is, and Saturn is more than another world—than ours or Earth; it is another system. His rings and his moons mark a complete system, distinct from the others, though chained to the distant sun by the power of gravitation. May it not be that solar influences, so potent with us, and still energetic in the Earth and Mars, here are weak, and that the planet himself has a force,—an independent existence distinct from the sun? We felt this in Jupiter; here it is more manifest."

"Had we not better secure ourselves first, and afterwards discuss these points? I see another of these strange, Saturnine monsters approaching us."

As he spoke, we turned and saw another huge being of extraordinary aspect rising from the morass and making towards us. We loosened the anti-gravitating force, and rose into the clouds. Here, poised in mid air in the Saturnian atmosphere, we watched the wondrous scene. Night was coming on. The sun, small and cold looking, was sinking in the clouds. It was a very different sort of day to yours or ours. The only thing I can liken it to was the short, dark day of a North Russian winter. But it was not cold. From the planet itself there rose a heated steam, evidently the result of its internal fires—a world yet not half cooled, such as yours was in the carboniferous age of the coal-shales.

As night closed in, the scene grew more than ever grand. Seven of the eight moons were in sight. Titan was at his full, Japetus was half-moon; Mimas, Enceladus, Rhea, were in the first quarter; Dione and Tethys were at the third. This alone—this galaxy of splendid moons—would have made a wondrous spectacle. But there was something still more marvellous. Like a huge yellow comet (only such a comet was never seen by man), from the eastern horizon to the western, stood the huge arc of the rings. It might be also likened to a rainbow, but more firm and solid in aspect, and not of many colours. The chasm between the rings came out clearly, and between them the stars could be seen. We floated on in this wondrous spectacle over the vast world, the glorious rings and the seven moons giving light (for seven only were in sight) to the strange scene of heaving oceans, and here and there low islands clad in mist and cloud, of that strange world. Night soon passed. Again the sun rose to give a clear light to that singular spectacle, but still a dim one compared to that which you and we have. Soon after sunrise, however, the great banks of cloud hid him from our eyes, and we were enwrapped in mist. We resolved to rise out of this. Using our anti-gravitating power, we rose once more into clear space, and then, beneath our feet, for hundreds of miles, we saw the vast clouds rolling around the mist-clad planet, much as, on an overcast day, the aeronaut sees the earth clad in cloud. We flew on hundreds, nay, thousands of miles, but still nothing but cloud was visible. The planet and his vast oceans and morass-like islands, and the strange forms that moved through his forests, were all lost to view. It was a huge cloud-land.

CHAPTER III.

RETURN.

"LET us go back," said Ezariel. "We have left a world of love and beauty to behold one of terror and wonder, where all seems unsympathetic to our nature. We have no place here. Happiness calls us home. We have seen enough."

Arauniel was at first inclined to make a still further plunge into space to the great world of Uranus; but I agreed with Ezariel that we had evidently passed beyond the regions where our nature was in place, and that it would be well to go no further. We had seen enough of the wondrous works of God to satiate our desire of knowledge. "Let us go back," I said. "We have seen enough. We have no place here."

So once more we mounted in our ether-car and plunged into space, and looked for many long days in wonderment still on that marvellous system of worlds and rings that we had left behind and never wished to re-visit. By degrees it sank into the sky and grew amalga-

o

mated into one planet; by degrees the great sun regained his glory.

We had long passed the orbit of Jupiter, when suddenly we perceived the force of gravitation drawing us toward a strange-shaped planet, or world rather, which suddenly appeared near us.

" It is one of the planetoids," said Arauniel. " They are not all spheres like the other planets. They are probably fragments of some great ancient world destroyed in primæval time, or else broken pieces of a huge ring that once circled our sun, like the rings we have just seen around Saturn."

We drew near to it. I cannot well describe it. More desolate than your moon, more terrible in its desolation. Vast mountains, waterless, treeless, huge masses of rock, coagulated blocks of star-forming matter—nothing living or moving. We rested on it some days and wandered on its strange cliffs, and then plunged off again into the orbit of the gorgeous planet Mars.

" Shall we not visit the earth ? " said Arauniel. " You have seen it, but we have not. Perhaps we may find on it some things which you have not seen."

" If you so resolve," I said, " you must indeed beware that men do not find out who you are. I kept my secret well, and only to one man did I quite reveal it, just before I left it for our home. If you do not keep your secrets, and if men find out who you are, you may lead them into sin; some will be ready almost to worship you; some will mock and deride you; some will brand you as imposters; in the end they will quarrel over you, and then you will lead them into sin, and thereby your-selves will fall and offend God."

"Then let us land in some place where men are not, and yet where we can see some of their works afar—say on some mountains in a fertile and cultured region."

"I can only think of the Alps," I said, "as a place suited for us. From them you will see a part of France and Italy and much of Germany. Men will not trouble you and you will not trouble them, for you need not go near their cities nor their haunts. If they find you amidst the snows and glaciers, you can flee from them and hide yourselves in the great fastnesses that man has yet never trodden. If we go from Alp to Alp, we may see a great deal and have a fair idea of Earth. But I warn you, go not into the haunts of men. One might do it and be unknown, as I have been; we could not all do so."

"Good," said Arauniel, "let it be so. We will

land upon the earth, but avoid men. We will see the works of man from the mountains and afar, and gather what we want of the natural wonders of the earth in spots untrodden by man. So be it, as you say—let us make for the ' white spot on the little continent,' "—for so we call the Alps, as ever snow-clad. We directed our ether-car towards the earth. Again I saw the familiar lines of the continents and oceans expanding before me—again I saw the lights of Earth's cities. We directed our course to the tall, white cliffs of the Jungfrau. At length we reached them, and once more I stood upon the rocks of Earth, amid the ice and snow and rock of Europe's greatest mountains. My first thought was to send to you this narrative of my journey. May it encourage you to lead the higher life on earth, that in another state of being you may be found worthy to know the glories of the heavens.

If you wish to see me again, come to Jungfrau, to the place marked, on the 26th, at sunset.

ALERIEL.

At the bottom of the page I noticed a map of Jungfrau with a place marked by a cross. I looked at the page, I rubbed my eyes, " Is it true or a dream?"

PART VI.—CONCLUSION.

CHAPTER I.

CONSIDERATION.

" I SHOULD like to go," I exclaimed.

" Oh, don't," exclaimed Maud. " It is a long journey to Switzerland, and,"—she paused —" and I do not like these supernatural beings, if they really are such. I do not like anything above this earth. Perhaps it is a mere imposture. If so, you would show yourself a mere fool to go ; if it is not, you will be utterly in their power. Do not go ; I believe it is all nonsense, after all. Don't go."

Her arguments were convincing. I thought over it. No, I would give it up. It might be, as she urged, a mere trick of a designing man, or a dream of some maniac.

Next morning, when the subject had been slept over, and I had just been working out some practical scheme of business, Maud, looking up from her work, said :

" If you are going to Switzerland, I wish you would take me with you."

" But, my dear, I have given up all thoughts of going. It is an imposture probably, or a delusion of a very eccentric man."

" I should like to ferret it out," she replied. " I wonder what it all means. Do these statements suit what astronomers have really found out about the planets ? "

" As far as I know they do. But, for all that, I think it a mere delusion of some person, who perhaps has learnt something about science."

" If there is anything in it, surely it would be worth seeing some one from another world, even if one went to Switzerland to see him."

" Well, my dear, but what is the good of it ? The probabilities are against it ; and, beside that, you were opposed to my going last night."

" So I was ; but give me the privilege of my sex. I am full of curiosity about these curious beings. I wonder what they are like."

To make a long story short, I yielded. I made arrangements for going away. Our things were packed, and in a week from the receipt of

the mysterious packet, we were *en route* for
Switzerland. We crossed *viâ* Newhaven to
France, and then from Dieppe went to Paris.
There stopping a day to rest, we proceeded *viâ*
Dijon and Dol to Neufchatel, and thence to
Berne.

CHAPTER II.

JUNGFRAU.

WE got to N——, on the slopes of Jungfrau, about noon on the 26th. We lunched at a little *auberge*, and then climbed up the slope, pretending that we were merely on a walk, and refusing a guide. Without much difficulty we reached the spot pointed out by Aleriel on the map. After some three hours' walking, we sat down on a rock waiting the sunset. Slowly the orb of day sank to the west, amid the glorious mountains. The rosy tints of sunset were just beginning to adorn the peaks, when I noticed coming towards me a figure wrapped in a large cloak, who, as he drew nearer I saw must be my mysterious friend.

"Oh, I am so frightened," said Maud, seizing my arm. "There he is. I wish we had not come. I wish I had never persuaded you to take this mad journey."

"Do not fear, dearest ; all will be well. God

is overhead, and will protect us. Besides, there is nothing evil or unkind in this strange being."

"I am glad you have come," said Posela, for it was he. "My friends would like to see you before they leave Earth. They wish to see a man before they quit this world. And thank you, madam, also for coming. They will be glad to meet you," he added to Maud; "you are as welcome as your husband. Follow me."

It was easier said than done. The ascent grew more and more difficult, and in some parts rather dangerous. Aleriel had to help us in several places; but he said nothing, and I was really, I must own it, too awed to trouble him with questions. The scenery was magnificent, but terrible. The sun had now set, and the Alpine peaks were tinted with rose light. This grew dimmer and dimmer, till the cold, white snows stood out against the black night sky. Still we followed our mysterious guide up the mountain side.

At length, getting anxious, I said, "Is it much further? It is dangerous to be on Jungfrau in the dark, and it soon will be dark."

"We have almost arrived. Descend this gulley."

He pointed to a small depression in the

mountain side, almost full of snow. We, following his direction, glided down into it some
thirty feet.   Then he led us a few yards up the
ravine, to a vast snow-pile, and pointed to an
opening cut in the snow.   Taking Maud by
the hand, he led her towards it.   She entered
with him, and I followed close.   A metal door
stood in the snow.   Aleriel opened it.   A blaze
of light came from within.   Maud, who was
in front, and thus could see more than I, gave
a sudden scream, and fell backwards fainting in
my arms.   What could it be?   As yet I had
seen nothing but the light.

Aleriel took from his breast a phial, and
poured a few drops on her lips.   She revived
almost at once, crying out, "Oh, do not go in!
They are dreadful—so unearthly!"

"Who?" I said.   "Let me see."

I leant forward, and once at least in my life
I beheld a scene plainly of another world.   It
was a small room, encrusted all over with
crystals of every colour and strange ornaments
in curious designs.   It rose into a little dome-
shaped roof, in the centre of which blazed a
powerful electric light, which made all around
glitter.   On the walls were fixed a dozen or so
curious instruments of a nature quite unknown
to me.   In the dome there fluttered a large

eagle, which had evidently been alarmed at Maud's cry. But this was not the curious part of the scene. On the side of the room opposite to the door were two strange beings with large wings, but who, I noticed in a moment after, were somewhat human in aspect, with faces full of intelligence and of calm expression. On their breasts were brilliant gorgets of jewels of divers colours, and down to their feet hung long robes of metallic tissue, richly embroidered in singular designs. It was indeed a combination of the bird type of life with human, or more than human, intelligence.

They looked at us as if with curiosity and interest, and then each waving their hands (for they had hands, unlike the avine tribe) over their heads in what looked like a gesture of greeting, suddenly burst forth together in a short song of welcome, soft, sweet, and enthralling. It had a most weird and unearthly effect. They seemed utter foreigners to us in every sense,—in nature, in language, in mode of greeting ; in fact, they evidently were not of the earth earthy.

" This is our mode of greeting a stranger," said Aleriel. " Every nation on earth has its diversity of customs, surely another world must be distinct from earth in all things."

I bowed to the mysterious beings, and
entered the jewelled room. Maud stood at
the threshold still awe-struck, but I beckoned
her to come in also. It was truly an unearthly
scene. I never realised till now how perfectly
and cleverly Aleriel had disguised himself to
seem so human.

I looked around me. All was quaint and
unearthly, but, for all that, beautiful. Crystals
of every tint glittered around and about me in
curious and quaint designs. Everything looked
different to what we are accustomed to see. It
was impossible to conjecture what some things
were for, and why they were so made. It was
evident that nothing there was earthly, or
made by human hands.

"You are cold," said Aleriel. "We can
easily warm the car. All the forces of nature
are under our command here."

So saying, he touched a metal knob on the
side of the vault. In a moment a warm breath
seemed pouring down upon us from above. I
looked up and saw two of the ornaments in the
roof glowing at white heat, apparently under
powerful electric action.

There was no seat in the room; but Aleriel
took two downy couches and laid them at our
feet, bidding us repose there, and, as he did so,

one of his strange companions, reaching up, unhung from one of the ornaments a large ruby vase full of grapes and bread, and, walking across, offered them to Maude. She shrank at the approach of the strange being, and turned to me as if for protection. I thought to myself, " No human power could protect us here if these strange creatures, with their wonderful command over the forces of nature, chose to injure or kill us." I felt how powerless humanity was in such a company.

Aleriel noted the shrinking, and consoled her.

" Do not refuse our friend, Ezariel. You have never had the opportunity before of receiving from the hands of a being of another world the fruits of earth. That vase I brought from the great ocean-capital of Mars. So see three worlds, the triad of which earth is centre and largest, are here joined together. The giver is from Venus, the fruits of Earth, the vase from Mars. Accept, pray, his refreshment."

She took the fruit and bread. He offered it to me, and I accepted it also.

CHAPTER III.

A NIGHT WITH UNEARTHLY FRIENDS.

"WOULD you like to retire?" said Aleriel. "You must be tired. I have prepared a couch for you here in this cabin, from which I have moved our instruments."

He touched a glistening crystal ornament at the side of the room, and instantly a sliding panel rose in the wall, disclosing a small cabin where some cushions were laid, covered with rich, but quaint, ornaments of fine embroidery. The cabin looked comfortable, and gorgeously, though eccentrically, fitted.

"Do let us go back," whispered my wife, "it seems dreadful to spend the night with these extraordinary beings. I would rather sleep in the meanest *châlet* on the slope than in this place."

"Why should you fear us?" said Aleriel. "What have we done or said to make you think that we would harm you? We would injure no one. Still our ways, even our life, is

not the same as yours, or under the same conditions. So, if in any way you are distressed,
say what you wish, and we will obey."

We retired to the cabin, and were soon asleep
on the soft couch. I awoke, however, after the
first dose, by my wife calling me. "I am so
faint, I feel suffocating. What can the matter
be?"

"I feel the same," I said. "The room is
hermetically sealed: Ho! help!" I called, as
I staggered to the door, and knocked at it.

A soft song answered. I tried the various
crystals with which it was embossed. I could
not open it, so I knocked more forcibly. It
seemed a matter of life and death, for really, if,
as it appeared, the room was without ventilation, we must shortly be suffocated. A soft
song replied. I knocked again. "Do let us
have some air. There is not ventilation enough."
Again a soft song. I knocked still louder. Then
instantly the panel parted. I saw the two unearthly friends of Aleriel standing in the outer
domed room, looking towards the cabin. He
was not there. They knew, as I was aware, no
earthly language. I could only make a sign to
my mouth, and draw a long breath to imitate
breathing. The air in the outer room was
purer, but still it was warm and close. How-

ever, actual suffocation was not risked there. I tried to make them understand we needed ventilation, but they could not comprehend me. I thought it best for us mortals both to go into the open air and breathe awhile. They thought evidently, when I made for the outer entrance, I wished to leave them. However, by gestures I made signs we would return. They touched then the outer panel, and, wrapping ourselves up, we passed into the fresh, cold, mountain air. It was a glorious, clear, starry night, and the white, snow-clad mountains loomed majestically around us.

Having both recovered from faintness, we returned to the outer vaulted chamber. Arauniel, it seemed (for that, I understood, was the being with the silvery wings and great jewelled star hanging from his neck), had understood my pointing to my mouth as a symbol of need of food, so he had got ready for us a large green vase filled with what looked like some dried fruit. But, though really we were both rather hungry—seeing our supper of bread and grapes had been a very light one,—we were afraid to eat.

"It may be poison to us, if it is food to them," said Maude. "Oh, do not eat it. It is evident there is a danger of their killing us, even without meaning us any harm."

" That," I said, " perhaps was the reason that Aleriel got for us the bread and grapes from the village. Still, the perfume of that food is very grateful, but I am afraid to eat any of it."

It was a strange position to be in—on this earth, in company with beings, though so singular, seemingly good, and certainly benevolent to us ; yet fearing to be killed at any time accidentally, from the simple reason that our human life was linked by a thread too feeble for them to comprehend. I thus realised how impossible it would be for a man to exist, even if he could get there, in the condition of our earth-life, on any world but this of ours.

Aleriel entering soon dispelled our anxiety. I mentioned my trouble at once to him, and he quieted us by saying that he had lived long enough on earth to realise the conditions of our earth-life, and that there would be no danger from our being left alone, as he would not depart from us while we remained in his ether-car. He opened with a burning bar a hole to ventilate our cabin. We retired to rest again, quieted by his assurance, and refreshed by some more provisions which he had procured us from a *châlet* not far off.

CHAPTER IV.

EXPLANATIONS.

NEXT morning we breakfasted in strange company. We tasted a morsel of the singular perfumed food which they had supplied, and which Aleriel said he was sure would be harmless. It was most agreeable to the palate. Our meal was made, however, of the simple provisions he had got and a little coffee. No animal food was offered, and I imagine he felt scruples in procuring it. At the beginning and end of the meal our hosts, with strange but solemn and impressive gestures, sang with exquisite sweetness a short hymn. After breakfast, Aleriel said :

"Arauniel is very anxious to ask you some questions about the earth, and I shall act as interpreter. May we put them to you, and record for our friends, to bring home with us, the sound of your voices in the phonograph ?"

I consented at once, and he placed a phonograph (of a different form to ours) near my mouth. For some five hours I then had a strange series of questions put to me, which I answered as best I was able—some of them relating to topics about which I had never thought, and which I honestly believe (having done a good deal of variorum reading) never yet have been discussed on earth. Others were far simpler, but I found a great difficulty in making my replies understood. Especially in religious questions I found this difficulty. None of the three evidently could understand how, if Christianity witnessed so strongly to the doctrine of love, Christians could so quarrel with each other on religious topics. That any one could be angry on religion none of them evidently could understand. It was an insoluble problem. They said that if people are in error we should feel pity, not anger; that truth could not be manifold, but one; and that passion must tend to encourage error, rather than to destroy it. Then they passed on to another mystery—the origin of war. They could not see why or wherefore men should try to hurt, or, still worse, to kill, one another. Surely there was enough misery in the world without adding to it? This led to politics. The political divisions of Europe, the quarrels of nations and their mutual jealousies, the different forms of government, even the diversity of languages,—all seemed to them very mysterious. On every matter they not only asked me what was the case on earth, but why things were as they were. As I, like most people, had taken things much as I found them, the causes of our social phenomena were very puzzling. In not a few matters, when pressed hard, I had to reply, that all this must be the result of sin, and of man's Fall, and if men were better things could not be in such a state. I must own it was painful to give these strangers so unfavourable an idea of humanity and of our earth, but there was no help for it.

Then we turned to other topics—to the mysteries of Nature, to the laws of death, and pain, and disease. Here new difficulties arose, and I had again to plead the Fall and man's sin. It seemed they knew of no pain, only under certain unfavourable circumstances, *e.g.*, on Saturn, or amid the burning regions of Jupiter, they had felt a certain difficulty of existence ; pain—localised pain—they had never felt. I found, however, they were not sure that they would under all circumstances be secured from death, or rather " would have to seek a new form of corporeal existence," as Aleriel put it ; but they always had evaded this by precautions, and by their intense and renewable vitality.

CHAPTER V.

ADIEU.

AT length I was physically wearied by the conversation, which required all my concentrated faculties to follow. I felt that if my object was to defend the state of society in our world, I had a bad cause. Maud tried to help me here and there with bright woman's wit, and to explain things I could not make clear. Our weariness was noticed by our hosts, who got us a refreshing mid-day meal, and Ezariel offered us with it, in an emerald goblet, a strange but most exquisite liquor, which entirely recovered us both, and the invigorating effects of which we felt for weeks after. Then we renewed our conversation, and so talked on till late in the afternoon, when I said that we must go if we would reach the inn before sunset. They made no objections, but said in an hour they meant to depart from earth. Our farewell was as strange as our meeting, and I felt a certain regret—I know not how to express it—

at parting with those who appeared so good
and happy, and who had tried to be so kind to
us.   Ezariel and Arauniel both accompanied us
to the door, and, giving each of us a small ring
of crystal as a keepsake, raised a sweet song of
blessing ; and each according to their use, as
it seemed, touched us on the forehead.   A
solemn thrill passed through me.   Then we
turned half unwillingly to descend the mountain,
Aleriel leading the way.   We soon reached a
beaten path, and then Aleriel also bade us farewell :

"God bless you both, and may we meet
again in a happier world."

So saying, he parted from us, remounting the
declivity.   A few minutes after I heard a
sudden explosion, as it seemed, in the mountain, and felt a rushing gust of wind.

"They are gone," said Maud.   "I am glad,
now, I have seen them.   It was like a glimpse
of heaven."

NOTES.

"Hark! there is the boom of the cannon." The cannon at the siege of Paris could be heard distinctly by day and night at Pontoise. I remember hearing the artillery from Mont Valerien myself during the second siege.

"I have often looked on England from afar." An island of the size of Great Britain would be distinctly visible in powerful telescopes on Mars or Venus. Indeed, many islands visible on Mars are probably no larger than our "tight little island."

THE MOON.

"I selected one large meteor." This may sound fantastic, but accepting the conditions given, *i.e.*, of a being of immense vitality and power over natural forces, is not irreconcilable to astronomical observations. The number of meteors is calculated.

"Boiling water was nothing to it." The calculation of the heat of the moon is higher than I have given.

"The absence of snow." There appears to be no snow,

nor rain, nor even water, nor atmosphere on the moon. What looks so ice-like in the telescope is merely (it would seem) the bare rocks glittering in the sunlight.

"Tycho." The metropolitan crater of the moon. His diameter is estimated.

"So I went forward . . . . to the great circle of Copernicus." The following eloquent description from "The Moon," by Nasmyth and Carpenter, may be worth quoting, as showing how some of our descriptions are not exaggerated. "Let us choose, for instance, the hillside of Copernicus . . . As hour succeeds hour, the sunbeams reach peak after peak of the circular rampart in slow succession, till at length the circle is complete, and the vast crater-rim, fifty miles in diameter, glistens like a silver-margined abyss of darkness. By-and-by appears a group of bright peaks and bosses. These are the now illuminated summits of the central cones, and the development of the mountain-cluster they form henceforth becomes an imposing feature of the scene. From our high standpoint, and looking backwards to the sunny side of our cosmorama, we glance over a vast region of the wildest desolation. Craters, from five miles diameter downwards, crowd together in countless numbers to the surface,—as far as the eye can reach looks veritably frothed over with them." "The Moon," pp. 164, 165.

VENUS.

"Whence the mighty Alps." This description is not imaginary. I saw it in February, 1872, more than once in the neighbourhood of Lake Biehne. I have often thought since that it admirably represented the way Mars appears to us in a good telescope, and, possibly, Venus, *i.e.*, a world wrapt in mist, with a projection here and there, and openings in the clouds. A somewhat similar arrangement of clouds I have noticed from the Dartmoor Tors. It is probably common in all mountainous districts.

I find that Fontenelle says of the " inhabitants of Venus," that they would be " loving music, inventing fête-days, dances, and tournaments." It is natural to suppose this lovely planet bright with love and joy ; but I have supposed the love of the higher spiritual kind.*

The reasons which led me to assume the bird type to be dominant on Venus are the following :—

1. The dense atmosphere of the planet ; probably one of the densest and most extensive in the solar system.

2. Its mountainous state, unfit for walking animals. Such mountain regions would be more fitted to bird than mammalian life.

3. Lastly, the apparent suitableness of the lovely bird-type of life to the Queen of Beauty in the heavens, revelling in that glorious blaze of sun-light. In spite of Swedenborg, unless proof were attainable to the contrary, I should like to think the creatures living on the fair evening star to be beautiful and joyous and good.

---

* Fontenelle, " Pluralité des Mondes." 1783.

Venusian.

I must also apologise for the word " Venusian."   I know
well that compounds ought to be derived from the genitive,
Veneris ; but these are already connected with ideas opposed to those I wish to convey.

Mars.

The ideal of vitality on Mars appears to be that as Mars
is so like the earth in (1) geographic configuration, (2)
climate, thus possibly its vitality is like that on earth.   I
have supposed it nearly the same at least in higher intelligence, only more near to the higher mammalia, *i.e.*, the
carnivora, than on earth, on account of :—

1. The tradition of the ancients of Mars symbolising
War.

2. Its Arctic climate.   The carnivora, *e.g.*, the bear and
dog dominate in earth's Arctic realms.   If there were a world
in which the Arctic element dominated, it would be one in
which the carnivora might be supposed to be supreme.
The idea of a lion or bear being endowed with reason is not
so ridiculous.   The former was called the king of beasts, and
there is a school of German naturalists who regard the bear
as nearer man than other animals.

In Mars we see an older world than that of this Earth,
and thus I have ventured to suggest there a more advanced
state of society, heir of *all* the ages, and thus something—
like what human society may tend—if progress is healthy.
The differentia of nature, however, the fiercer Martian
character, I have tried to preserve.   It has been suggested

to me by a friend that this part of my "fairy tale" is like
Lord Lytton's "Coming Race." If so, the resemblance is
accidental, or rather Bulwer and I have, from observation
and induction, come to the same conclusion.

The nomenclature of Martian lands I have used is the
French system of M. Flammarion.

JUPITER.

The question among astronomers now is whether life can
exist on the largest of the planets. Most regard Mars and
Venus as probably peopled (it may be with higher intelligences than earth); but the recent discoveries, which tend
to show the great heat of Jupiter, are urged against the
largest of the worlds around us being peopled. It is almost
manifest that this huge world and Saturn cannot be peopled
by beings like men, or our higher land mammalia; but this,
I contend, does not hinder the existence in those huge
oceans of Jupiter of beings like the monsters of the deep,
somewhat similar to the cetiosauri or ichthyosauri of our
ancient seas, or the whales and dolphins of our own times.
On earth the two main conditions of abundant life are heat
and moisture; on Jupiter and Saturn both of these appear
to be in excess. If life can exist on these heated oceans, it
must be somewhat as M. Flammarion and I have supposed.
If such a life as I suggest is not there, then there either is
none, or beings of a totally distinct nature to what we can
conceive.

As to Saturn, the conception of an invertebrate being of
intelligence is one that seems monstrous at first; but, as
Brewster says, "Is it necessary that an immortal soul
should be united to a skeleton of bone, or imprisoned in a
cage of cartilage and of skin? Must it see with two eyes

and hear with two ears, and touch with ten fingers and rest on a duality of limbs? How many possible forms are there, which eye hath not seen, nor the heart of man conceived." These strange forms are to us grotesque, but not necessarily impossible.

P. 203. "They had hands unlike the avine tribe." As the most serious objection I met with in my "Voice from another World" was to the supposition of vertebrate beings existing with three pairs of limbs, I venture to quote Professor Owen on this point : "We have been accustomed to regard the vertebrate animals as being characterised by the limitation of their limbs to two pairs, and it is true that no more diverging appendages are developed for stature, locomotion, and manipulation. But the rudiments of many more pairs are present in many species ; and though they may never be developed as such in this planet, it is quite conceivable that certain of them may be so developed, if the vertebrate type should be that on which any of the inhabitants of other planets of our system are organised." *In some fish, if I mistake not, there are more than two pair of limbs. As to the question of muscles, the amount of vital force, if increased, might generate strong muscular action without large muscles.

---

* Owen "On the Nature of Limbs," p. 83.

THE END.

WYMAN AND SONS, PRINTERS, GREAT QUEEN STREET, LONDON.

www.ingramcontent.com/pod-product-compliance
Lightning Source LLC
Chambersburg PA
CBHW020111030726
47498CB00006B/2045